Katie's Plain Regret

KATIE'S PLAIN REGRET

AMISH JOURNEYS ∼ BOOK 1

Sara Harris

WordCrafts

This book is dedicated to my grandpa and favorite Texan, Bull. You may have been Just Bull (J.B.) in that classroom so many years ago, but you'll always be a hookin' bull to me.

Chapter 1

Gasthof Village, Indiana
1890

As the sun sank lower in the sky and the farther she got from the safety of Gasthof Village, each step on the rutty clods seemed to hurt more than the last. *What were you thinking, Katie Knepp?*

The cool Indiana breeze that had been kissing her ankles and cheeks switched direction without warning, whipping her covering strings across her lips. Somewhere in the distance, her mother's pitiful moans and hysterical shrieks were still audible.

"I'm sorry Mama," Katie whispered, batting the troublesome strings from in front of her face. She hadn't known what to expect when she told her parents she was leaving their safe and secluded world, bound for the wilds of Texas, but she certainly hadn't expected her mother's reaction.

"Don't let my baby go, Jeremiah," she'd screamed as Katie descended, like a whipped pup, down the hand-laid wooden porch after delivering her news. In atypical Amish fashion, her mother had made a dive for her from the top step, only to be expertly intercepted by her father. "Don't let her leave us! She's likely to get killed, Jeremiah. Don't let my baby go."

The stone-like expression of her father's bearded face and empty, broken eyes haunted her mind, giving her a shiver down her backbone. Something told her she'd never see her beloved parents again. Still, she had to go.

A sudden burst of wind sent the covering strings lashing across her face again. This time, they stung. "God, please comfort my mother and give her heart peace over my decision. Help her to understand that I consulted You in prayer before even considering this journey."

Carefully, she tucked the taxing strings into the nape of her hand-sewn dress. *I could just take my covering off and stow it in my apron,* Katie thought.

Guilt at simply having the thought niggled in her stomach. Even though she was well away from the watchful eyes of her Amish village, it still didn't feel right to take the white gauzy prayer covering off completely. She gave it a pat as another of what was most likely her mother's shrieks met her ears. "God, please hear my prayer—"

As quickly as it gusted, the breeze died off, leaving Katie alone in a vast and eerie calm. The yip of a coyote replaced the melancholy laments of her mother, now lost without the breeze to carry them. Instantly, a choir of yips encircled her with their echoing sounds. Katie froze and scanned the world around her. Nothing was out of place and there wasn't one tell-tale tail, or much less a hair, giving rise to any suspicion of her stumbling into the midst of a pack of coyotes.

The sky to the west was a splash of pastel colors and a shudder raced down her spine as the incessant yipping continued in varying octaves. Glancing over her shoulder, Katie pointed her nose skyward into the falling darkness and let out a lingering howl. At once, the coyotes silenced before filling the skies with a chorus of haunting howls in answer.

"What beautiful music they make," Katie mused, continuing

down the trail and pushing thoughts of her brokenhearted mother down deep in her soul. From seemingly nowhere, a gray pup scampered across the trail in front of her. Its fluffy body seemed too large for its tiny head as it paused and looked at her through wide, wild eyes. Then, stumbling over its too-large feet, the young coyote disappeared into the brush that lined the trail.

Katie giggled. "Go on silly baby. Go find your family, they're all around us."

She'd only continued a few more steps before the howls silenced and the feeling of being watched became almost too much to bear. As darkness deepened the sky's hue, Katie remembered the supper in her bag just as the whuffing sound of curious coyotes met her ears.

Icy fingers of fear clawed at her stomach as the feeling that came with the coyotes around her changed from strangely cheerful and probing to strangely hungry—and her feeling hunted. *Maybe I should just start for home now and forget any thought of Texas. If I walk quickly, I could even run, and I'll leave the food for these animals...*

Katie whirled on her heel, ignoring the yellow eyes that peered at her from the lengthening shadows. A low growl rolled out of the understory.

In the distance, a flickering glow caught her attention. "A campfire," she cried. Plunging her hand into her bag, Katie produced the venison steaks her twin sister Annie had packed for her as she'd broken the news of her travels to their parents.

Heaving them behind her and not bothering with the biscuits or pie, she ignored the snarling and snapping that ensued almost immediately and took off at a dead run toward the flickering salvation on the horizon.

"Welcome Miss, won't you come and join us?" The English woman's smiling voice was almost as warm as the fire when Katie burst into the camp unannounced. "Coyotes are awful bad tonight. Heard tale myself that they're being driven north from the devastating drought down south. Hungry things, they are." The kindly English woman held out a dented tin plate to Katie. "Have you eaten darlin'?"

Katie shook her head and accepted the plate. A sudden, foreign popping sound from suffocating darkness behind them made her jump.

"I'm Michaela. Michaela Dawson. That's my husband Jake and son Logan you heard there."

Confusion narrowed Katie's eyes.

Michaela grinned. "They're keeping those pesky coyotes at bay." Her blue eyes, wide with curiosity, sparkled in the firelight. "What may I ask are you doing out on the trail, all alone at night?"

Tears burned the back of Katie's throat. "I'm Katie Knepp. My family lives back up the road a bit in Gasthof Village."

Michaela nodded, filling her plate with a ladle of beans. "Ah yes, the Amish settlement." Plucking up a fork, she sat down on a long log and motioned for Katie to join her. "Do you need a ride home, Katie Knepp?"

Taking the proffered seat, Katie shoveled in a forkful of beans, suddenly feeling the effects of her trip in her growling stomach. The beans were gritty, as though they'd been cooked beneath the Dawson family's covered wagon as they traveled throughout the day. Forcing the bite past the lump in her throat, Katie struggled to remember her manners. "No ma'am, but thank you. I'm headed south." Her voice cracked a bit. "To Texas."

Michaela's eyebrows arched skyward. "Is that so? Well, best of luck to you. Mess of problems down south. If the bank robbers don't get you, the grippe will." She chugged a drink from a silver cup. "We're headed even farther north, to Montana, ourselves. Inherited a cattle ranch." She drained her drink and let the cup dangle between her knees. "We have until the end of the month to claim it, otherwise it goes to the next of kin. That rich old goat wouldn't know what to do with a cow other than fart around and get himself stepped on." Shaking her head, Michaela continued. "He'd wind up getting mad at his own incompetence and selling off the whole ranch before he even realized what he had." She smiled, breaking her tanned face into a freckled mess of weathered wrinkles.

Michaela couldn't have been much older than her own mother and she had an inviting air about her. With her long almond colored hair tied back in plaits beneath a straw hat and a denim skirt that reached her ankles, Michaela looked the part of an English cattlewoman.

Another popping shot, closer this time, sent Katie's plate of gritty beans into the dirt at her feet. "Oh, I'm so sorry," she stammered, scrambling to pick up what she could salvage, hear heart pounding in her ears. "I would offer to share my dinner with you to make up for my dropping yours, but I haven't any left that aren't crumbs."

"It's alright Katie, I'll get you more," Michaela said, ladling another helping of beans onto a clean plate. "You seemed mighty hungry. Did you drop your dinner on the trail?"

Katie dug into the heap of grainy beans. "No ma'am," she managed through the mouthful of beans. Finally, she swallowed. "I threw it."

Michaela cocked her head, sending the shadows from the firelight bouncing across her angled features. "Really?"

Katie helped herself to another heaping bite. "When those coyotes surrounded me, right before I saw your camp, I figured they smelled the venison my sister packed for my dinner. So I gave the steaks a fling into the brush. And ran."

Slapping her leg, Michaela let loose with a whoop. "You *fed* the coyotes? My dear girl, you're lucky they didn't eat you alive!"

Katie pondered this as she cleaned her plate. "But they'd already had my steaks, what would they want with me?"

Michaela sobered. "Katie, you feed them and they associate you with food. How long do you think it'll take a starvin' coyote to figure out a human and the food from a human are the same thing?"

Katie shrugged, feeling supremely ignorant.

Gently, Michaela continued. "In its mind, wouldn't take much to make the human the food, way I figure it."

Michaela's logic sank like a stone in Katie's gut. She began to shake.

With a reassuring pat, Michaela began again, not giving her time to respond. "Don't worry darlin'. You'll ride with us into Elizabethtown. And I'll give you a new bag, one that doesn't smell like a coyote's dinner. Once we arrive, if you are still of a mind to get to Texas, I'll buy you a ticket on a railroad and lend you our scout, Johnny Tyler. He's due to meet us in Elizabethtown tomorrow. That way, I'll rest easy knowing you made it to your destination safely."

Katie summoned all of her manners and mumbled a thank you while struggling to keep her eyes open. Michaela led her to a bedroll beside the fire and began to sing. *A strange song,*

Katie thought, as she drifted off to sleep. Something about a colored rose in San Antone.

His face, fuzzy in its dreamlike state but still handsome as ever, filled her sleep-heavy mind. The blue-eyed, dimpled face with the fading scar through the eyebrow, framed by those blonde waves that shone golden in the sunlight whenever he removed his felt hat. Peter. The face she'd hoped to wake to every day for the rest of her life, for as long as God saw fit. *Her* Peter.

If only he had proposed forever. Katie's heart ached deep in her chest, despite it only being a dream. "Peter," she whispered, longing pulling at the end of his precious name. "Peter."

His mouth, upturned at the ends ever so slightly, began to move. "Katie."

On some level, she knew she was on the verge of tears. They burned in her throat and blurred his already fuzzy face even more so. "Oh Peter, I miss you already."

Somewhere nearby, an out-of-place coffee pot clanged against a rock. Katie could feel herself trying to wake, but fought to stay asleep. To stay with her Peter. More foggy now, Peter's fading face just smiled his trademark patient, knowing smile. "Stay with me," she rasped, emotion evident in her throaty words.

Peter's mouth began to move again, giving rise to his disjointed and strangely echoing response. "I love you, Katie Knepp. No matter where you are. I love you."

A flash of heat surged in her core as her mind fought to awaken to the newly dawning day. "Then why didn't you ask me to marry you? I might have stayed… for you." But Peter was gone.

Katie's eyes fluttered open. Across camp, Michaela was

starting breakfast while her two fearless coyote hunters snored from their nearby bedrolls. Homesickness washed over her, a sob catching in her throat. Katie turned her back to the happy familial scene and let the salty, cleansing tears soak her cheeks.

Chapter 2

Elizabethtown, Illinois

"Y ou still going to Texas, Miss Katie?" Logan Dawson's voice was muted as they pulled onto the main street of Elizabethtown, Illinois. Michaela's son, who couldn't have been more than a year or so older than she herself was, had to be the most striking Englishman she'd ever seen. With piercing blue eyes, dark blonde hair, and a wit as sharp as her pa's old ax blade, Logan had certainly garnered her attention. He had a little swirl of hair on the crown of his forehead that was a perfect letter 'o', and when he removed his hat, it stuck straight up and made Katie giggle. It was no secret to anyone in the Dawson's wagon party that she had caught Logan's attention as well.

She took in the view of clapboard buildings that lined Main Street. In varying shapes and sizes, they sat behind a long, tumbledown boardwalk that seemed to lead straight out of town, right into the wilderness. Without warning, her thoughts shifted to Peter.

Sweet Peter, who was hands down the best-looking man she'd ever set eyes on, English or Amish, filled her mind. Though easy to look at, it had been his compassionate heart that made her long for his proposal—the one that never came. A discontented half-smile found its way onto her lips. "Yes Logan. Yes, I am still going to Texas."

Logan removed his hat and ran his free hand through his hair. Katie peeked from the corner of her eye to check his swirl. Just as she figured, it stuck straight up and kind of curled over at the tip, like an ocean wave. He'd volunteered to drive the wagon into Elizabethtown, once it was decided that was where Katie was going to be riding. "That's too bad. I was hoping you'd accompany us on up to Montana Territory."

Katie felt scarlet creep into her cheeks as Michaela rode up beside the wagon. "I was hoping we could entice you to come along with us, as well." She smiled, big and broad. "Katie darlin', if Texas don't suit you, wire me at the Powder River Ranch in Montana. I'll send fare for you to join us, and you can try your hand at the cattle trade."

Jake piped up from somewhere behind them. "I was hoping you'd come with us too, Katie. I'm mighty tired of eatin' beans every meal, and was hoping you'd make us something different!"

Turning in the saddle, Michaela threw a mock-angry look at her jovial husband. "Very funny, Mr. Dawson."

Logan pointed down the road. "Hey Ma, ain't that Johnny Tyler there, coming out of the—coming out of the *saloon?*"

"Some folks never learn," Michaela muttered as she spurred her horse and dashed ahead of the wagon.

By the time Logan and Katie had parked the wagon and climbed into the street, Michaela was in the midst of giving Johnny a good tongue thrashing. "You hired on to scout for the Dawson family, Mr. Tyler. Not wind up drunk in a saloon."

Johnny removed his hat and ran a hand through his thick, black hair. "Beggin' your pardon, Mrs. Dawson, it's my money and I'll spend it how I see fit." No doubt feeling Katie's innocent stare, he met it and flashed a flirty wink.

The color in Michaela's cheeks was like none she had ever seen before. Carefully, Katie broke eye contact with Johnny and examined her hands in her lap, feeling as though she'd done something wrong by watching. *She's leaving me in his watchful care to get me to a train station?* Katie shuddered.

Jake strode up from behind them. "I have the horses all set at the livery. Mr. Tyler, I've heard enough. You're dismissed." He flicked a coin though the air, which Johnny let land in the dirt at his feet. Turning to Michaela, Jake didn't miss a beat before continuing. "I'm going to procure us a new scout. Rest up now." Tipping his hat to Katie, Jake strutted off down the street, obviously in as high a temper as his wife.

Logan began unloading the goods from the wagon and placing them on the boardwalk in front of the hotel. "I'll book us a room, Ma. I'll get you one too, Miss Katie."

With Johnny lingering in the background, Michaela faced Katie. Tenderly, as though she were her own daughter, Michaela placed her hands on Katie's shoulders. "First thing you gotta learn when dealing with the folks that ain't Amish, Katie, is when they show an aptitude for the drink, you gotta turn 'em loose. No good can come from a man, or woman, who's up to their neck in booze all day long." The color had faded from her cheeks, leaving the bright smile and friendly wrinkles. "This isn't the first run in we've had with Johnny and whiskey. Last time he sold the horse we bought him and got himself thrown out a saloon window. So we were out the cash money for the horse, and the window to boot." She paused. "I'm sorry you had to see that."

Logan stuck his head out of the door of the hotel. "Rooms are ready Ma, Miss Katie."

"I understand, Mrs. Dawson. Thank you for all you've

taught me, and for the new bag." Katie smiled. "I won't be storing steaks inside or feeding coyotes from it, I promise."

"Good girl," Michaela said, giving her a squeeze about the shoulders. "Let's get you inside where you can rest. I won't be entrusting your wellbeing to Mr. Tyler, as you probably assumed, but don't worry. I'll leave you in capable hands."

Katie tried not to meet the stare of Johnny Tyler as Michaela guided her into the hotel, but when he noticed her peeking at him from beneath her covering, he winked again and flashed a suggestive smile.

Ignoring him and the strange brand of knots that had turned up in her stomach, Katie dutifully followed Michaela and Logan into the hotel.

After a nap, Katie awoke refreshed. Though Michaela had offered to treat her to dinner before her family pulled out of town, Katie didn't feel right accepting any more financial hospitality from them. Donning her covering, she ignored the glass mirror in the corner of the room and made her way downstairs. *Now, to find a way to make my own money to pay for my expenses. Thank goodness Mrs. Dawson bought me a train ticket. Spending another night running from coyotes isn't the best way to get to Texas.*

Stepping into the twilight street, Katie immediately caught sight of a marvelous glass-windowed store front. On the glass itself, fancy green letters on gold covered it entirely.

MINERVA'S DRESS SHOP
CUSTOM ORDERS WELCOME

"It looks like they're still open," Katie mused, stepping

across the muddy dirt street. She gasped as she stepped inside the dimly lit, luxurious store. Dresses of all colors lined the walls. Some resembled the hues she'd seen in rainbows. The rack in the middle of the room, however, boasted dresses of colors that, to her, had no name. Fabrics she'd never seen, not even in New York, made up the merchandise. Borders and edgings she'd never known existed lined the hems, waists, and cuffs of some of the dresses. Near the back, beneath an elegant candelabra, stood three giant mirrors, all angled in. Throughout the store sat chairs of all shapes and sizes. But not chairs like she'd sat in before. These were soft-looking, fluffy, and just begging to be sat on.

An array of objects festooned the walls. Some looked to be drum-like, others were smaller bells. A tiny pair of what looked like cymbals hung behind the counter. Without thinking, Katie stepped forward and fingered the sleeve of a deep purple dress. She'd never felt its equal. "Oh my," she began, feeling more and more of the dresses that hung nearby.

"Those dresses are my newest, I make them myself. They are velvet. I am Minerva." Stepping from the shadowed back room, a foreign woman, looking to be in her early forties, appeared before her. Wearing a green and gold dress just as strange and wonderful as the ones on display, Minerva held out her hand. "Welcome to my store."

Katie felt her jaw go slack. "Um," she stammered, awkwardly taking Minerva's hand. "*Hallo.* I'm Katie, Katie Knepp." Standing next to Minerva, whose long hair was as dark as night and eyes emerald green, Katie suddenly felt very out of place. "Forgive me Minerva, I'm in the wrong—no, I just shouldn't be here."

"God leads us places for a reason," Minerva said, smiling.

She gestured widely with one arm. "Please, take a seat. Let us talk."

Katie eased down onto a purple velvet chair, which really seemed more of a large cushion. Minerva sat opposite her in a matching purple cushion-chair. "What brings you to these parts, Katie Knepp?"

Feeling more at ease, Katie relayed her dreams of Texas, her sorrow over leaving Peter, the heart-wrenching tale of leaving Gasthof Village and her parents, and the handsomeness and strange attractive quality of young, English Logan. When she finished she drew in a long, deep breath. "Minerva, may I ask you something?"

Minerva smiled, revealing two perfectly straight rows of gleaming white teeth. "Certainly."

"I haven't seen many different kinds of people, but I have never seen anybody like you. Are you, well, English?"

Ducking her head, Minerva grinned bashfully. "Oh sweet Katie. Here in America, you are American no matter your language. My family hails from the Roma people. Some here call us Gypsies. I came here when I was young, during the War Between the States." The flickering candles gave a nostalgic and haunted feel to the story. "I married twice, both to—as you call them—English men. Both fought for the North, but my brother-in-law fought for the South." Slack jawed, Katie interrupted. "Married… twice?" The thought was as absurd to her as being eaten by coyotes.

Pausing in her spiel, Minerva arched an eyebrow. "Married twice and widowed twice. But I have two beautiful children to show for it, a boy and a girl."

Katie grinned back at Minerva, thrilled to learn that her story had a somewhat happy ending.

Minerva smiled back. She shook her head as memories washed over her sending her wavy ebony locks cascading over her shoulder. "This is where I met my first husband, right up the river at Alton Confederate Prison."

Katie's eyes widened, but before she could ask any more questions, a tiny bell rang from the direction of the door.

"Ah, a customer. Last one of the night, too. Tell me, Katie," Minerva said as she rose gracefully out of the velvet chair. "Was there something I could offer you besides conversation?"

Katie studied her shoes. "I need a job, but I won't be in town long. Might you have any dresses I could mend for you?"

"Certainly. You wait here, I will bring you some." Minerva waved to the waiting customer before disappearing into the back room. After only a moment, she returned with an armload of dresses. "Here you go, Katie. Bring them when you are done and I will pay you. You'll find a sewing kit in the pocket of the top dress."

A wonderful heat rose into Katie's cheeks. "Thank you, Miss Minerva. I'll have them done and returned as soon as I can." Katie bit back her excitement as she strode toward the door.

"You're welcome." Minerva answered with a smile as she turned to greet her customers. "Charlotte, Cotton! What a welcome surprise. Come in, sit awhile."

Katie dipped her head into a nod as she passed the pair of customers. The handsome young man with the deeply tanned skin and the tall woman with eyes as green as the shopkeeper's, greeted Minerva with a hug as Katie let herself quietly out the door.

It wasn't hard to see what needed mending. A loose button here, a piece of fallen lace there, a misaligned hook and eye closure every once in a while. By the time her candle had burned down halfway, Katie had already made a considerable amount of progress on the pile of dresses.

Sitting back in the straight-backed chair, she let out a sigh. "Okay, only four more to go then I can return them to Minerva in the morning." Plucking up the needle, she took aim at a loose cape button on a silky, yellow house dress. A pounding at the door made her miss the button and stab her finger. "Who could that be at this late hour?"

Glancing out the second-story window, Katie noticed the action from the vicinity of the saloon. "Mrs. Dawson was no doubt right about liquor," she muttered as she opened the door a crack. There on the other side, slumped against the frame, was Johnny Tyler.

Locks of greasy, black hair hung in his face, outlining his wicked grin. Beneath his stained shirt hung a gun belt, made complete with two gleaming silver six-shooters. His pungent aroma was a nauseating mix of exotic perfume, cigar smoke, and whiskey. The stench was so strong that Katie covered her mouth and nose with her hand, before she remembered her manners.

"*Hallo*, Johnny. You seem to have lost your hat." Katie replayed the words in her mind, realizing just how silly she sounded.

Johnny's wicked grin spread wider and he straightened his back, pulling himself to his full height. "Why Johnny," he mocked, apparently trying to be funny. "You lost your hat!" Laughing alone, he appeared not to need Katie to have a conversation. "Ain't she just so cute. And sweet. No doubt a maid, pure as the driven snow." Something terrifying clouded Johnny's eyes, then cleared.

"If you'll excuse me, I'm really quite busy. G'nite." As Katie went to push shut the large door, Johnny stuck the toe of his boot in, just before it closed. Katie chewed her bottom lip as her heartbeat quickened to a gallop.

"I understand you're trying to make some money 'fore you leave town." Hefting his weight against the door, he shoved past Katie easily. As he passed, he caught her wrist with his filthy hand. "I know a way I might can help." He cackled sardonically. "You got something I want and I'm willin' to pay two dollars for it."

Katie gently turned her wrist. *If he can't feel me pulling away, he may not realize I'm not here until I'm already gone.* She glanced at the open door and considered screaming. Before she could open her mouth, Johnny slapped his other hand over it. "What, two dollars ain't enough? It's the goin' rate—and too much in my opinion."

Without stopping to think, Katie jerked her wrist free and clamped her teeth together hard on the soft flesh of Johnny's palm. Before he could let out the string of curse words that no doubt were coming, something swooshed down and landed on Johnny's head with a resounding thunk. Johnny slumped to the floor.

Shaking, Katie turned back toward the door. There in the doorway, standing almost as tall as the door frame itself, stood Peter. He flipped the wooden garden trowel in his hand. "Looks as though being a farmer is good for something."

"Oh, Peter!" The tears came quickly as Katie rushed into his waiting arms. "Oh, Peter, oh thank you, God. Thank you, Peter!"

He circled her in his muscular grasp, holding her as though

he'd never let her go. "All this adventuring certainly never leaves you without needing rescuing, Katie," he murmured into her hair.

Pulling back slightly so as to look into his eyes, Katie sniffled. "Why did you—how did you…?"

Gently, Peter placed a finger to her lips. "If you had waited just a minute before leaving my place after telling me of your wild Texas scheme, I had gone in to fetch Ma and Pa. I wanted to talk it over with them, so as we could all come to a conclusion together. But when we came out, you were already gone."

Katie moved back into Peter's embrace and rested her cheek on his chest.

"So, we talked and made some decisions. One of which was to lend me the buggy so I could come after you. Katie, you are a hard girl to track when you get moving." She could hear the smile in his voice as they swayed slowly together, back and forth.

Peter patted her back. "So I followed you, found where you fed the coyotes your dinner before joining up with the Dawson family."

"I don't have any stories left to tell you, Peter. You seem to know it all." Katie sighed, exhaling the weight of the English world that had been accumulating since leaving Gasthof. "But how did you know their name was Dawson?"

Peter released Katie from their embrace and guided her over Johnny, helping her to sit on the bed. "Well," he began as he turned back to the pile of drunk on the floor, "Michaela, spritely woman that she is, hired me to escort you to the train station in the morning." Hefting Johnny onto his shoulder, Peter carried him easily out of the room.

Katie twisted her feet together on the wooden floor and swiped at her mouth. Johnny's hand had tasted dirty and sour. A moment later, Peter returned.

"Where did you put him?"

Grinning, Peter gestured toward the window. "In the horse trough outside."

Katie rushed to the window. "Peter, won't he drown?"

Stepping to her side, Peter guffawed. "Worried about him, are you? Silly girl, look."

Peering out the window, Katie saw that Peter had in fact put Johnny in the horse trough. Body submerged and still unconscious, Johnny's head and arms hung out one side of the trough and his legs the other, giving the thwarted outlaw the appearance of soaking in a bath.

Katie covered her mouth with her hand. "Oh my!"

Peter caught her free hand in his. "I wasn't done. Sit down."

Unused to Peter being strict, Katie complied and wasted no time in nestling herself in between the piles of dresses.

He knelt on the floor before her. "Since I was hired to take you to the train station, I thought you might like some traveling company the rest of the way." His eyes, stormy and green as the sea of New York's harbor, stared into hers.

Katie's lips twitched into a smile. "I would."

"Then I will." Peter paused. "On one condition."

"What's that?"

Sweeping her hands up in his, he spoke solemnly. "We travel together with none of the pressures we had in Gasthof." Standing, Peter swooped Katie into a hug before she could answer.

When he sat her down, she nodded. "Alright, Peter Wagler."

She held on to the hug longer than usual, holding him close to her and breathing his scent.

"I think it's high time we got you to bed."

Scarlet rose into Katie's neck at the mention of bed. Immediately, she let her arms drop from their embrace. Though she was happy to have Peter traveling with her and his promise to get her safely to Texas, she hadn't intended on sharing a room with him or leading him on to believe she wanted to do so.

Before she could speak, Peter leaned down until his breath was warm on her ear. "I'm right next door if you need me." Softly, he brushed her cheek with a kiss—their *first* kiss.

Raising her hand, she cupped the side of his face before he could pull away. "Thank you Peter. For everything." Before she could think of a reason not to, Katie leaned in and, wrapping her arms tightly about his neck, pressed herself against him in a passionate embrace. Fire coursed through her veins as she let herself be overcome by the sensation of what it would truly feel like to be Peter's wife.

When their embrace ended, her face burned. "It's an answered prayer that you're coming with me," she whispered, her voice cracking. "I missed you."

Stepping out the door, Peter patted the trowel on the dresser. "I'll just leave this here, in case you need it." He chuckled at his own joke before pulling the door behind him. Just before it closed, he peeked back in. "Oh, and Katie? I missed you, too."

Morning came much too soon. Groggily, Katie managed to pull herself out of bed when the sun's rays were still short on the floor. As she was just fastening the cape of her dress about her shoulders, an incessant knock came at the door. Katie snatched up the trowel that she'd slept with and inched toward the door.

"Katie it's me, Peter. Open up!"

Flinging open the door, Katie discovered a very awake Peter, who looked to have been up for hours.

Stepping in, he bent and brushed her cheek with another sweet kiss before sinking into the straight-backed brown chair. "Do you want the good news or the bad news?"

Katie eased herself onto the bed. "Eh, the good news."

"Looks like we'll be traveling together in my parent's buggy to Texas. You like buggy rides, right?" He managed a half-smile.

Katie crossed her ankles. "Yes I do, and I'm glad to be traveling with you. But doesn't it make more sense to take the train?"

"That's the bad news. Michaela left money at the station for you to buy your own ticket. I suppose she wasn't sure when you were going to be leaving town."

Katie pondered this a moment, watching the dust motes float down lazily to the floor through the rays of sun. "Why is that bad?"

Peter was silent until she met his gaze. "Katie, the train station was robbed this morning."

Chapter 3

Illinois

"**R**obbed?" Katie looked the teller. His little hat was flat on top with a wide brim, which cast a long shadow over the curve of his familiar face. The face she didn't know she'd missed. Until now. The din growing behind them from other thwarted passengers made Katie square her shoulders. The silver dollar, pressed into her hand by Minerva only minutes before, was heavy in her dress pocket.

"Yup," the spindly man replied. He no doubt had related the same message to countless people before her, and it showed in his choppy voice. "A group of fellers who called themselves the Wild Bunch came whoopin' in early this mornin'. Thanks to them, train's not comin' back through till they're brought to justice, or until further notice."

Katie glanced into the ensuing bedlam that surrounded them. "The Wild Bunch? Now that's a memorable name for a group of outlaws."

The teller smirked in disgust. "Memorable? Ha! Nothin' memorable about them bunch of hoodlums, if you ask me. Just like that Butch feller that leads 'em. He's got a hefty bounty on his head."

"Bounty?" Katie's interest was piqued.

Peter leaned to whisper in her ear. "Hush up, I'll explain later."

Wide-eyed, the teller stared at Katie. "Girl, they didn't just rob me of the depot money. They robbed *you* of a ticket." He adjusted his wire-rimmed eyeglasses and peered at the line that had grown behind them. "I'm sorry, no refunds. Next!"

"Excuse me, sir," Peter interjected. "Can you tell me the easiest route to get to Texas?"

The attendant huffed. "You plain folk drive buggies, don't you?"

Peter nodded.

"Then I suggest you take the stagecoach road." He removed a pencil from over his ear and pointed out the window. Framed in the precious glass was an empty railroad line which led south. "Since the bandits done been through, you two should be safe. At least for a while." He huffed again. "Next!"

Peter ushered Katie out of the line to the tune of grumbling passengers left stranded without a train to board. "You wanted an adventure, Katie Knepp. It looks like you've got one. We're taking the stagecoach road by Amish buggy."

"Do you think we'll see a real stagecoach, Peter?" Katie craned her neck out the open buggy window. They had only pulled out of Elizabethtown a few moments before, but already a foreign emotion fluttered in her chest like a caged bird.

Peter flipped the reins. "I reckon so, at some point. Bandits are holding up trains, not stages." He glanced over at Katie. "Are you alright? You look like you're about to jump right out of here."

Katie turned to face him, her hands knotted in her lap. "I can't rightly explain it, Peter. I'm so excited that I'm doing this—little Katie Knepp on the adventure of a lifetime." Her cheeks ached from grinning. "But I'm so scared at the same time I don't know whether to look this way or that, fear this or fear that. The unknown is so—fearfully exciting!" Heart pounding in her chest, she turned her attention from Peter back to the buggy window. "Maybe we'll even see a *bandit*."

Peter chuckled. "You're quite an elemental woman, Katie. It takes the real things in life to keep you happy. Adventure, emotion. The mundane everyday will never suit you, will it?"

"Mmm, elemental. Yes, that's it." She flashed a grin at Peter. "Are you elemental, also?"

A dry wind swirled up from the south, spinning and spitting dust inside the buggy. Peter squinted and coughed. "I reckon so. I certainly wouldn't give up this lifestyle for anything. After all, through you and your family, I found God." He flicked the reins again and continued as easily as though he were talking about what kind of pie to have for dessert. "You can't get much more elemental than the Amish. Learned so much from you and your folks. Found where I'm supposed to be, where God *meant* for me to be. But I'd be lying if I said I didn't miss the very things you're coming to love on the trail. The adventure."

Katie stuck one of the strings of her covering into the side of her mouth and pondered this a moment. "Peter, if you loved the lifestyle so much, why didn't you stay there?" Realizing the harshness of her words, she sputtered over a quick apology. "Well, what I mean is, how could you leave Simon and Sarah Wagler? After they adopted you into the village, good and proper?"

Peter studied the road ahead of them as it rose and fell with the gentle hills. "I thought you'd never ask."

Katie fiddled with the damp covering string and sucked

in her bottom lip. "I suppose I have been a bit preoccupied Peter. I'm sorry." *God, on a trip I hoped would bring me closer to You, I am already failing. Please help me be the person You want me to be.*

Peter smiled. "I don't want your apology, Katie Knepp."

What do you want? Katie bit her tongue before the question flew off with the same brand of reckless abandon that was becoming more and more commonplace whenever she opened her mouth. "Then why did you leave it all behind to come with me?"

Peter gave her a sideways glance, careful not to turn his attention too far from the road ahead. "I never got to finish telling you, did I?" His voice was thoughtful. "In addition to talking to Ma and Pa, I had to tie up some loose ends at Gasthof or I'd have been by your side the moment you stepped off my porch."

Katie's cheeks burned.

Pretending not to notice, Peter continued through his own shy smile. "My ma and pa will be joining us down in Texas, Katie. Pa and I talked about a furniture store when they took me in. Neither of us wanted to intrude on Samuel Stoll's woodworking business in Gasthof, though." He straightened his back and looked hard at an out-of-place noise in the brush.

Katie was silent as she watched him study their surroundings. When she could stand it no longer, she let her words slither over her teeth with a quiet hiss. "Is it a bandit?"

Peter didn't answer, but didn't turn his attention from the brush, either. After a moment, he continued in a whisper. "Some of the elders, as it turned out, weren't very keen that I made it through my year-long probation. Everyone seemed fine with me joining the community when the whole mess of the Wagler's adopting me was brought up. As it turned out, some wished I would just disappear and not taint their secluded world with anything remotely English."

"Really?" Katie ticked the Gasthof Village families off on her fingers. *Who could have said such a thing?*

"I don't blame them," Peter went on. "The Amish way is beautiful and maybe they were right." He pulled back on the reins, stopping Sookie, the buggy horse. "Maybe I'm not completely able to cut ties from the English world. I certainly followed you at a moment's notice, didn't I? My thirst for adventure is still as ripe as the day I walked onto the Stoll spread in Gasthof."

Insides quaking, Katie offered a shy smile to the man who'd come to save her.

"Katie do you still..." Peter started. He swiped at the perspiration that gleamed around his mouth with one hand. "What I mean is, I know you wanted—at some point—to, well, what I mean is, do you still want to..."

Standing up in the buggy, Katie pointed down the road. "Peter look! Here comes the stagecoach."

Sure enough, the stage had just topped the hill in front of them. "Lucky for them the bandits have already come and gone, just like the station teller said," Katie mused. "Not much protection out here in the wilds."

No sooner were the words out of her mouth, than a shot echoed off the hills. From both sides of the road, bandits descended upon the poor helpless stage. The fellow riding shotgun for the stage flew off the seat and tumbled in the dirt.

"Was that a bullet?" Katie asked, unable to quell the excited note in her voice. "I have never seen one before!"

"Katie, sit down," Peter commanded. "If we're lucky, they

were focused on the stage and not on us." Carefully, Peter eased the buggy off the road into the brush.

"Why don't we go on and turn back, Peter," Katie asked, her words coming hard and fast. "But that man, shouldn't someone go check on him?"

Peter looked at Katie as though she were speaking a foreign language. "Of all the fool things Katie," he began. Instead of finishing, he dropped his voice to a whisper and started afresh. "Not everyone in this world is good. We'll do the best we can by the man hurt, if we're lucky enough not to have been spotted." Peter shifted his gaze to the fracas just in time to see the driver throw down his weapons and the cash box. The bandits were already relieving the passengers of their items when Peter continued. "If we're going to make it to Texas, Katie, you're going to have to start using your head. We can't turn back, we can't go forward. We have to sit here and wait—and pray we weren't spotted."

Katie recoiled as though Peter had slapped her with his words. Never before had he spoken so harshly to her. Mentally licking her wounds, Katie focused on the scene playing out before them. She watched as the men, bandanas obscuring their faces, hopped on their horses and readied themselves to be on their way. Forgetting to be hurt, Katie spoke more loudly than she intended. "Peter, look! The bandits are leaving."

Peter's eyes widened. "Katie, shush!"

Grinning, Katie pointed toward the stagecoach road. "There, I think we're safe." The surge of adrenaline brought an almost audible thump to her chest.

The click of a weapon at her ear though, brought a cold knot to her throat. "Come on out here," hissed a voice from behind them. "Both of you step on out of that buggy."

Katie obeyed, eyeing the bandit warily. Chunks of greasy black hair curled out from under his dirty hat. A bandana, which probably had been blue at one time, hung limp over the bottom half of his face. Turning his attention from Katie, he pointed the weapon at Peter. "I said move it, dude."

Peter stared hard at the stranger as he folded his tall body out of the buggy, his face tensed into a mishmash of planes which made him almost unrecognizable to Katie. As scarlet crept up Peter's neck and into his face, she could almost see the prayers flying from the top of his head. *Probably praying for patience*, she figured.

From the corner of her eye, Katie caught sight of a trembling woman outside the stagecoach. A shift in the breeze brought the grandmother's lament to her ears. "My late husband gave me the wedding ring they took. That was all I had left of my sweet Clyde McDougal."

The man who'd been riding shotgun on the stagecoach seat pulled himself off the ground, one hand holding his injured shoulder. Moving at a snail's pace, he dragged himself to the elderly woman's side. He no doubt spoke words of comfort to her, but his words were lost on the breeze and still the old woman was inconsolable. Hunched in stature, she gave over to a crying jag. Her thin shoulders shuddered as the waves of emotion swept over her again and again.

To steal an elder's memories of the love that filled her life. Katie bit her cheek as an emotion she hadn't known that she possessed rose up from the depths of her very being. Rage heated her face and brought a tremble to her fingers. *Those folks were as innocent as the day is long. I should be scared, God, I know I should. The bad Englishmen have found us.* She glanced at the bandit. *But I'm not scared.* Her chest began to heave. *I'm mad.*

"Both you plain folk turn around and hit your knees," the bandit demanded through his dirty bandana. His weapon still pointed precariously at the pair of them as he turned his face to the understory. "Jim, I got some more over here!"

A charged prayer wracked Katie's brain as she stared at the cowardly bandit. *Dear God, thank you for this adventure. I am sorry it has to end this way. Please comfort my parents. Since I'll be meeting You shortly, please forgive me for bringing Peter into what may send him to meet You, too. Also, please forgive me in advance for what I am about to do.*

Peter did as he was told and melted to his knees. Katie glanced at him, red tinging her vision. From the look on his face, it was obvious that Peter knew what was coming as much as she did.

Standing her ground, Katie stared hard into the icy eyes of her would-be killer. "No, I will not hit my knees. And I will not turn around."

Peter craned his head to look at her. "Katie, do as he says. Now."

Ignoring him, Katie kept on. "You take what isn't yours. You hurt, you leave sadness and hopelessness and fear wherever you go." She shook her head incredulously as though the bandit had asked her to turn water into wine. "No, I will not kneel for you. I will kneel for God, the one who made both you *and* me. I will *not* kneel for you, not now. Not ever." Tilting her chin up, Katie steeled her jaw. "You are God's child too, you know. And He loves you."

The bandit stared at her as though she'd lost her mind. It was the same look Peter had worn earlier when he'd looked at her. Slowly, the masked man lowered his weapon. "I thought you plain folks weren't supposed to talk?"

Katie softened her gaze, ignoring his off-handed comment. "Hasn't anyone told you before that God loves you? Ask Him to walk with you and He will. But right now, with the terror you're inflicting to these poor people who had done nothing to you, you are breaking God's heart."

The bandit's voice came out in a soft, husky whisper. "No one ever told me no tale of God before."

"Not even you parents?" Peter asked, rising to Katie's side.

He shook his head. "Nah, they died. These fellows are my family now."

"Never too late to get in touch with God," Peter said. "Only knowed him a year myself." He glanced at Katie. "And it has been by far the best year of my life."

The bushes shuddered a moment before another masked man stepped forward. "What's all this?"

"Oh Jim—I was just, uh—" The bandit trained his weapon on Katie and Peter again. "I was—"

Jim's voice was even more gravely and sinister than the first man's had been. "I told you to scour these hills and dispatch any witnesses."

"Don't feel right to shoot two Amish folk, Jim. They didn't hurt no one."

In one whoosh, Jim drew his own pistol and whacked the first bandit across the face. "Well if you ain't man enough to do it, I am." Leveling his weapon at Peter, Jim pulled back the hammer.

The scream ripped from Katie's throat so quickly, it felt as though it left a trail of blood. "No!"

The sudden boom of a discharged weapon silenced them all.

Missouri

God, *please take Peter into Your loving arms*, Katie prayed as she slowly dared a peek through one watery eye. However, both of her eyes widened at the scene which lay before her.

Jim and the bandit Katie felt she had almost led to Salvation stood with their quivering arms held high above their dirty hats. A streak of blood trickled down Jim's right hand before disappearing into his shirt. The weapon he'd drawn on them was nowhere to be seen.

There, sitting tall on a horse before the lot of them, sat a young man. "You look like you fellows could use a hand," he said, a silly grin tilting his lips at an awkward angle on his freckled face. He was tall no doubt, and not much older than Katie and Peter.

Actually, Katie thought, *he may even be a bit younger than me*. As he stared at them, his blue eyes sparkled with a certain brand of gaiety that only the youth can know. Three fellows rode up quickly behind him, dismounted, and began to tie and shackle the bandits.

"Got the rest of 'em down below, Bob," one mumbled through a wad of what Katie presumed was tobacco.

Still staring at Katie, young Bob pushed the brim of his hat up with his pistol before holstering it and swinging down from the saddle. "Why, howdy ma'am. I'm Bob. Bob Dalton.

Who might I have the pleasure of addressin'?" He walked with a swagger that put Katie in a mind of her old self-assured tomcat, Whiskers.

Whiskers had always managed to bring home the scrawniest mice and saddest of birds, but from his proud swagger, he seemed to think his prizes the most grand. Always delighted with his catch, it seemed as though he wasn't sure what to do with his prey once he got it back home. However that never stopped him from swaying along with the typical tomcat swagger, even when he would let his dinner go free and then try to befriend it. Katie would smile and set out a bowl of fresh milk for the big-headed stray that couldn't seem to bring himself to eat another living thing.

"Peter Wagler and Katie Knepp," Peter said extending his hand. Even though Peter spoke and Bob shook his hand, the young man's azure gaze was still trained on Katie.

Lifting his hand, Bob touched the tip of his hat. "If you'll excuse me ma'am, I have some outlaws to shake down and articles to return to their rightful owners."

Katie watched through the leafy canopy as Bob returned to his business. Still weeping, Mrs. McDougal was obviously overjoyed at having her wedding ring returned, however they sounded to be happier tears than they had been earlier. Offering her his hand, Bob assisted Mrs. McDougal back into the stagecoach, along with the other passengers. Holding up one finger, he examined the wound on the shot man's shoulder. Motioning to the stagecoach driver, Bob pointed up to Katie, but his words were lost on the breeze before she could make them out. The driver nodded at Bob, who promptly began walking with the wounded rider up to where she sat watching.

"Howdy there, Katie girl," Bob said as he meandered back into camp. She and Peter had lit a fire and tried not to watch as the men who'd ridden in with Bob Dalton interrogated the men that had held up the stage. Holding him by one arm, Bob helped the shot man to have a seat by the small fire.

"Was it the Wild Bunch who held up the stagecoach?"

Bob stopped and turned to face her, a puzzled look on his face. "I figured you to have a voice sweeter'n the mornin' dew Miss Katie Knepp, but I didn't figure you to know anything about the Wild Bunch." With a shake of his head, the confounded lawman went back to examining the man's injury.

"It went clean through, but you're going to need that hole sewed up back in town." Bob was adamant as he packed the hole in the old man's shoulder full of a bandana from his back pocket.

The stagecoach rider shook his grizzled head. "No way Mr. Dalton. I'll be fine. Ain't got no money to pay no sawbones."

Bob grinned and shot a wink at Katie as she took in the scene through wide eyes. "Ain't your debt to pay, Mister." Pushing himself up, Bob sauntered over to where the unmasked outlaws were shackled to a gnarled oak. "Which one of you was the shooter?"

Nobody offered an answer.

"That's just fine then," Bob said leaning over the outlaws. One by one, he rummaged a coin out of each of their vest pockets. "Thanks boys, this should just about cover the doctor's fee for the man you shot."

The wounded man grinned and offered a nod. "Many thanks."

His medical tending done, Bob turned his attention back to Katie. "So, tell me Miss Katie. What exactly does a little Aim-ish girl know about outlaws?"

Katie watched the injured cowboy saunter back to the waiting stage. He climbed back up to the shotgun position with a little help from the driver. After a moment, they snapped the reins and continued on their journey. Realizing everyone was staring at her, still awaiting an answer, she stole a quick glance at Peter.

He poked a stick in the fire, sending up a shower of orange sparks, but said nothing.

"Well," she began, "I know the Wild Bunch owes me a train ticket to Texas."

Bob pulled a biscuit and handful of beef jerky out of his knapsack. He offered the morsels first to Katie, then to Peter. Both refused the proffered food. "Well darlin', this here ain't the Wild Bunch." He grinned, giving his boyish features a mischievous look. "This here's the Burrows Gang, though incomplete. Rube and Jim Burrows were the two men who you and Peter there became acquainted with back up in the bushes. These two ugly fellows here are the Brock brothers. Looks like Henderson and Nep." He raised his voice a bit. "Those two idiots ride with your gang too, don't they boys?" He spoke to the outlaws, but didn't look at them. "Looks like those got away. Anyway, you're mighty lucky they didn't get their slick mitts on you. Every lawman in the country has been after this bunch at one time or another, and rumor has it that they don't treat pretty girls too kindly."

Peter bristled a bit. In the language only the pair of them shared, Katie whispered quickly. "I'll start us some dinner."

Retrieving what they'd brought in the buggy, Katie began a large meal. Before long, a fluffy tin of biscuits was ready, along with fruit preserves, honey, and stuffed crust rhubarb pie. All the while she worked, the hungry gazes of Bob and the bandits that made up the Burrows Gang were hot on her back. "So you're a lawman, Mr. Dalton?"

Bob smiled at her as Peter looked on while he tended the horses. The fact that Bob's gaze was never far from her brought a flush to her cheeks and knots to her stomach. From the corner of her eye, Katie noticed Peter watching Bob, his eyes hot emeralds. The look he was giving the young lawman was none too kind.

Bob smiled easily at Katie. "A lawman? No ma'am, I'm not that noble. The boys and me—" Bob gestured to the men at the edge of camp with tied-down holsters and empty eyes. "We're bounty hunters."

"What's a bounty hunter?"

Peter coughed loudly.

Bob gave him a sideways glance as his lips tilted into an awkward, crooked smile. "Miss Katie, you're mighty handy around a camp," he complimented, eyeing the pie. "I do believe it's time for us to get these fellows back to Elizabethtown, though."

The bandits licked their lips like hungry, misbegotten dogs.

Peter's voice rang out through the darkening camp. "Perhaps you all would like to stay and have dinner with us before you go? It's the Christian thing to do." To Katie, it sounded as though Peter was trying to convince himself of that, as well.

Without waiting for an answer, Katie dished up plates for both Peter and Bob. Not stopping there, she had dinner for all of the shackled outlaws plated before anyone could offer a rebuttal. "Would your, um, boys, like some too?"

"No they're fine, thank you," Bob said, not bothering to ask the looming men who hovered at the edge of camp. To Katie, they looked more like vultures eyeing a stumbling, sick cow than actual men. However, they had all managed to come along at just the right time to save both her and Peter from the clutches of the outlaws, so she couldn't think ill of them. "Many thanks to you, Miss Katie."

Katie took a seat next to Peter. "Will you be a bounty hunter forever, Mr. Dalton?"

Ducking his head, Bob tried to formulate an answer through a stifled laugh. "I don't reckon so."

"Is bounty hunting something you'll train your future sons up to be, too?"

Bob almost choked on his pie. "Why, no ma'am. Fact is, this here is my last job before I head out to Indian Territory to join my brothers, Grat and Emmett." He helped himself to a large bite and spoke through the crumbs. "They've got a security firm started out there, so I'll be helpin' them to run it."

Katie nodded, lost on all the nonsensical words.

"Need all the law they can get out that way, wild as it is," Bob muttered absently. "Miss Katie, if you don't mind my sayin' so, that was mighty fine pie and equally thoughtful of you to dish some up for the Burrows Gang." He glanced at her from the falling shadows. "However, you must have a cruel streak in you that not even my men possess."

Katie studied Bob's laughing eyes, glittering in the firelight. *What does he mean?* Turning, she looked at each of the outlaws' plates. Each had a biscuit topped with preserves and a generous slice of pie set before them on the ground. Then, it dawned on her. "Oh silly me! I didn't give them any utensils..." Katie's voice trailed off on the night winds as she scurried to gather enough forks for the men.

Bob let out a whoop that sent the night birds, those which had been singing in the tree overhead only moments before, beating the chilled night air with their wings in a burst of sudden, feathered urgency. "Why no, Katie, that ain't it. Those men are shackled, they can't reach the food you gave 'em, utensil or no utensil!"

Katie's smile melted from her face as she realized Bob spoke the truth. She had, indeed, set out heaping plates of food for hungry outlaws as they sat shackled to a tree. Helpless, she glanced at Peter. A smile, albeit tiny, had found its way onto his lips, too. He gave a little shake of his head as if to say, *Good job, Katie Knepp.*

Gathering the forks and lifting her skirt just a bit, Katie hurried over to where the outlaws sat immobile. "I'm so sorry," she said, plucking up the first outlaw's plate. "What's your name, sir?"

All the men, chained and unchained alike, looked at her as though she'd grown another head. Unsure of what to do, the first outlaw muttered under his breath as if he spoke a secret for only her to hear. "Willard Lenny, but they call me W.L." Before the last initial was clear of his lips, Willard opened wide for his first bite. Swallowing without bothering to chew, he opened his mouth again, like a baby sparrow waiting on a worm. In only a handful of bites, W.L.'s plate was bare. "Thank you Miss," he managed. The polite words came out rusty, like a forgotten door being opened for the first time in a coon's age.

Katie moved to the next man. "Well I be hog-swaggled," Bob swore from behind her. "I ain't never seen such a thing." Katie ignored him, focusing all of her attention on the hungry outlaw before her.

"I'm Leonard, W.L.'s my brother," he reported before letting his lower jaw sag like a hapless, oily rag. With the hint of a smile playing at her lips, Katie fed the man. His plate was clean in less time than his brother's. Dutifully, she moved to the first of the Burrow brothers.

"Hey," Bob interjected. "What do you say there Leonard? That lady didn't have to feed you and I certainly wasn't going to. You owe her a—"

"Thankee," Leonard grumbled.

Like a toddler being told to do something he doesn't want to do, Katie thought.

She nodded to the sulking outlaw before plucking up the plate for the first of the two men for which the outlaw band was named. "Hello Jim," she said before offering up a forkful of pie. "Figured you'd like your pie before your biscuit, just like the others."

Jim flushed and opened his mouth a tad. "Thank you Miss Katie," he whispered. "I'm mighty sorry we almost offed you and your beau back there."

Katie smiled softly. "There are better ways to make a dollar in the English world," she imparted over the emptying plate, "that won't cost you your eternal soul."

Hanging his head, Jim offered a slight nod. "Thank you, ma'am. I'm done. You can give the rest of mine to Rube."

Scooting over, she came face to face with Reuben Houston Burrow. "So what were you saying earlier, Miss Katie? About God?" He sat straight, his eyes glistening with moisture.

"Well Mr. Burrow, God loves you. He wants you to be happy and live a life that honors Him. He will bless you for it, too." She held up a bite of pie.

Rube accepted the forkful of pastry, never taking his eyes off Katie. "If you don't mind my sayin', Miss," he stated once his bite was swallowed, "we almost blew you and your man away back in those trees. How can you call that a blessing?"

Katie lifted the biscuit to his waiting lips. "It was a blessing meeting you, Reuben Burrow. And something kept you from, as you said, blowing us away. We met for a reason." Dropping her hands to her lap, she waited for him to chew the flaky biscuit. "And I got to share the good news."

"Good news?"

Nodding, Katie offered him the last bite of biscuit. "Yes, the good news of God's love for all men. And, I got to share it with a certain man who needed to hear it."

Reuben sniffled. "I'm mighty sorry, Katie. Sorry a girl like you is wrapped up in the likes of us." A lone tear dripped down his cheek as he chewed.

"What happened to turn you on a path away from God, Mr. Burrow?"

A handful of tears joined the first. "Yellow fever," he said, voice cracking. "Took my wife, only woman I ever loved. Left me with two babies to raise on my own. It weren't fair."

By now, Rube's testimony had the attention of everyone in the camp.

"So I left. Moved off to start a new life. Needed a new woman to tend my kids till my crops came in. Married up with a sweet young gal, but my crops failed. We was broke, so I turned to robbin' with these fellers here." He sniffled long and loud, the tears silently leaving dribbles down his cheeks.

Katie swatted absently at a fly as it buzzed the filthy outlaw.

Rube seemed not to notice as he continued. "When I come back from my first job, she left me. Took my kids too. Ain't never seen nor heard hide nor hair of any of 'em since." Rube ducked his head and gave over to a crying jag that was probably long overdue.

Katie's heart wrenched in her chest. "Just ask, ask Him for help. Your soul is hurting. He can mend it." Katie was on the verge of tears herself. *God please change this outlaw's heart—*

"While we're bein' honest, there's somethin' else. This here's Joe Jackson. He ain't my brother Jim." Rube sniffed and his voice cleared. "Jim died last year of consumption. He was in the pen when he died so every lawman probably knows, but guess word ain't made it to the bounty hunters yet."

Katie dared a peek at Bob, whose smile slid from his face, dripping into a deep frown. "I let the lady feed you sad excuses for human bein's. It's time now we get gone. You men got a train to catch."

Katie bit her tongue and rose to her feet, careful not to make eye contact with anyone. Bob's tone had changed so drastically, drips of icy fear danced down her backbone.

Peter gestured to the buggy. "Katie," he said softly, helping her inside.

Once she was safely out of sight, Peter stood guard, his arms crossed across his chest. Indeed, Katie felt safer with Peter between her and the moody Bob Dalton. Both watched inconspicuously as the bounty hunters loaded the bandits up on some strung-together horses. Their iron shackles clinked heavily as they started off on the trail back towards Elizabethtown under the cloak of darkness.

"Got a trial waitin' for you," Bob chided the outlaws. "Or a necktie party."

A necktie party?

"With any luck, the train you ride back to Arkansas won't get held up," another of the bounty hunters continued. "If it does, maybe this time you'll take the bullet you got comin' to you."

Katie climbed out of the buggy and took her place next to Peter. "What's all that?" She took care to keep her voice quiet.

"Lots of bad blood between those men. They'll be lucky to make it to Elizabethtown alive," he muttered absently, a faraway look in his sea-foam eyes.

Katie wasn't sure if he meant the outlaws or Bob and his men, but nonetheless, she listened to her gut and let the conversation go.

"Goodbye Katie Knepp," Bob called suddenly, turning in the saddle. His jovial smile was back, lighting up his young, freckled face. "If you're truly headed down Texas way, there's a bad drought. Fires springing up everywhere, so be mindful." The wink he flashed by moonlight made her stomach turn over with an odd thunk.

Offering a slight wave, Katie glanced at Peter who stared after the odd group of men, all of whom seemed a little ignorant of the law. His eyes grew stormy. "We did right by them. Nobody can say we didn't. But me," he turned to Katie. Those deep, green eyes cleared of the gray haze that invaded them when Bob was near. "I'm glad they're gone."

Chapter 5

Meramec Caverns
Outlaw Country, Missouri

Katie mopped at her brow with the sleeve of her dress. The heavy, dark blue fabric seemed to attract the heat. Before long, she'd have to do laundry. She stole a glance at Peter. Sweat gleamed on his brow as well. Still, he never once complained about the heat or the Amish clothing. In fact, he'd worn a tiny smile, most of the time, since the beginning of this journey.

"Where are we now, Peter?"

"Missouri. Kind of pretty, isn't it?"

The land that surrounded them was like nothing she'd ever seen. They were in the woods, no doubt about that, but the massive rocky outcroppings that peeked at them from above the canopy were nothing short of majestic. "This surely has to be God's country, as much as Indiana. Don't you think?"

Peter pushed up his hat as a rogue breeze swept a swirl of coolness through the buggy. Katie tipped back her head and closed her eyes, relishing the welcome chill.

"I'd say that's your answer," Peter replied, sucking in the draft. "God's country for sure."

Katie studied the giant walls of rock as they passed. Trees of every color dotted the ridgeline, no doubt hiding more adventures behind their leaves and branches than were offered down here on the stagecoach road. "What's a bounty hunter, Peter?" The question flew off her tongue before checking with her brain.

The smile faded from Peter's face. "It's been two days since we've seen any bounty hunters, Katie. Or outlaws. You're still thinking of them?" Peter dipped his chin until it almost touched his chest before snapping the reins over Sookie's back. "Or should I say thinking of *him*."

Still your words do nothing but bring hurt to those you love. Or those who love you. Nice job, Katie Knepp. "I got the impression that asking what a bounty hunter did was something that shouldn't be spoken of in their presence. But I know I can ask you anything." Katie knotted her hands in her lap. "I just want to know who we were dealing with is all." Her voice sounded meek, even to her own ears.

Peter has been there for me in good times, but even more faithfully in bad. She had agreed to marry him after she was baptized in the Amish church. However, it had never been clearly stated as to whether or not her failure to be baptized in the Church negated their engagement. Since they were breaking from the Old Order settlement of Gasthof, the rules were no longer clear. Katie jerked at her covering strings. *Everything used to be so simple. Maybe this trip will do nothing but bring hurt to everyone. Why did you have to cause such a ruckus, Katie?*

Peter's voice was equally mild when he finally spoke. "I'm sorry for speaking so sharply to you, Katie. Just a bit jealous, I suppose." The canopy of trees closed overhead as Peter continued, even more softly than before. "I saw the way Bob Dalton looked at you. He could have whisked you off to more adventure than you could stand. Enough to fill three lifetimes, no doubt. I half expected you to go on with him."

Fiddling with her covering strings, Katie looked everywhere but at Peter. "You never answered why you gave up everything in Gasthof to come with me."

Peter reined Sookie to a stop. "Now that's the easiest question you've asked today." He shifted. "Because I love you."

Katie's heart jumped in her chest. Peter's stare seemed to burn on her face, but still she couldn't meet his eyes. Those stormy, sea green eyes that had haunted her dreams until visions of Texas had pushed them aside.

Still Peter stared. "I'll always love you. As far as I'm concerned, leaving Gasthof didn't change anything. I still hope to marry you." He drew in a deep breath. "Someday."

Katie caught a twang on the word. "Someday?"

Peter's lips pulled back into a forced smile. "I came along to see that you made it safely to where you want to go, Katie. May seem that I haven't done such a good job so far."

I didn't want to say that.

Pausing just a moment, Peter stuck his hand in his pocket. "But so you know, I wasn't going to let those outlaws snuff us out." From his pocket, he produced a tiny little pistol. "I wasn't going to use it unless I absolutely had to. Luckily, Bob Dalton ensured this little knuckleduster remain a secret."

Hands flying on their own, Katie clutched at her throat. "Oh Peter, the Amish don't—"

"The Amish man," Peter interrupted, "would never let an outlaw just simply take the life of the woman he loves." He slipped the little .22 caliber pistol back into his pocket. "Or maybe I'm just not good at being Amish."

"Oh, Peter—" Katie gently laid her hand on his. A wave of

heat, not brought on from the horrendous drought, radiated up her arm.

"Don't say it. Don't tell me you love me and don't tell me you still want to marry me." Peter slid his hand out from under hers and snapped Sookie back into a trot. "I won't accept it until this trip is complete, and your wanderlust is satisfied."

Ooh, wanderlust. I like that word. "Alright, Peter. That's fair enough," Katie said to her lap. *God, again, please forgive your stubborn servant.*

Sookie's hooves had clipped along awhile before Peter broke the gentle silence again. "A bounty hunter kills men or takes them in to *be* killed. For a price."

Katie's brow knitted above her eyes. "For a price? They trade men's lives for—money?"

"That's how some men choose to make a living for themselves."

Katie felt a rush of sadness tug at her heart, weighing it down. "Why? Why would they do such a horrible thing?"

"They track down horrible people," Peter explained patiently. "Those with bounties on their heads aren't usually found in the front row of a church house."

Katie started to respond, but Peter hurried to cut her off.

Peter didn't look at her as the words rolled off his tongue, strongly and with a purpose. "Might have done it myself, on occasion."

Katie's jaw dropped lower than it ever had before. "Oh, Peter. Isn't that akin to murder?"

Peter shrugged. "I said life with the English was hard. I did things I wasn't proud of, but I turned from those ways and embraced your culture. And I embraced God for the first time in my life."

A haze hung over the southern tree line, catching Katie's attention as she pondered Peter's words. *God forgives when we ask Him to do so.*

"Would you hold it against me, chasing down men who do nothing but bring down the human race, and turning them over to authorities? Then being paid for doing so?"

Katie studied the haze as it grew thicker, tinging the sky a shade of wintery gray. A sharp, stinging odor curled into her nose. Slapping one hand over her mouth and nose, Katie reflexively grabbed Peter's arm with the other. "Peter—I smell smoke." *I suppose Bob Dalton was right about the fires, too.*

Moving quicker than Katie ever figured possible, Peter yanked Sookie to a halt and hopped deftly from the wagon. Speaking in slow and soothing tones, Peter took her by the bridle and led her off the trail. He glanced about only a moment before the mouth of the cave seemed to open up before them, right out from the trees.

"Thank you, God," Peter said loudly as he led both horse and buggy into the mouth of the massive cavern. "You certainly do provide for Your children, even when they don't know that they need it." Grinning, Peter trotted back to the buggy and extended his hand.

Heat rose into Katie's cheeks, but she took Peter's hand and stepped down.

"M'lady," he said with a devilish wink.

The heat burned hotter and began to course through her veins.

"Well, I suppose our friend was right in his assuming fires would be brewing down south," Peter said, removing his hat. His blonde locks were plastered against his forehead in almost perfect curls.

The sudden urge to run her fingers through those curls tingled in Katie's fingertips so fiercely that she clasped her hands behind her back. "Hmm?"

"It's a fire. Because of the drought." He flipped his hat back up to his head and pulled it down into place. "Well, what do you say we bring this buggy in as far as it can go and wait out the fire in the coolness of this cave?" Peter gestured over his shoulder.

Katie's mouth opened slightly. "Al—alright," she managed. Eyes wide, she took in the full, gaping expanse of the rock cavern.

Black soot marks dotted the back part of the cave and the walls. "Others have been here," she whispered, her voice full of awe. Curiosity taking over once again, Katie stepped toward the shadows that stretched forward from the darkest recesses, she examined every detail.

Tracing her fingers along the wall, Katie made it all the way to the furthest most point in the cave. "Oh Peter, come look!" Dropping to all fours on the damp cavern floor, Katie peeked around a camouflaged corner. "It goes even *farther* back. We just have to squeeze through here—"

Peter appeared at her side with a kerosene lamp. "Dark in there," he said with a grin. "Let's go exploring."

Peter went first, squeezing through the little opening with the lantern. Katie looked up as she made her way into the inconspicuous entrance. *The opening goes all the way up to the top. Hmm, it even opens up more up there.* Pressing herself through the crack, Katie shivered as she emerged into the absolute darkness. Stepping quickly, she joined Peter as he stood silently with his back to her. "Peter, I—"

"Shhh," he answered. "Just look."

The sight laid out before them made Katie rub her eyes. Peter could only gaze about the underground wonderland same as her. "It's like something right out of a dream," he muttered.

Or a nightmare. The cave room was large with giant, glistening spikes hanging precariously overhead and the light from the lamp cast a rainbow of colors in the gleaming rock forms. Drops of water dripped from every spike, creating a surreal musical experience that threatened to overwhelm her. "It's so large, you could hold a barn raising right here and never touch one of those giant spikes," she gushed. "Look, there's a lake over there." Katie took his arm, and they stepped closer to examine it.

Sure enough, rivulets of water cascaded down the wall and poured into a clear pool against the nearest wall. A fan of ripples floated from the wall in elegant, tiny waves. Peter held the lantern down closer. "You can even see the bottom. Here, hold this a second." Passing their light source off to Katie, he rolled up his sleeve. "I have to try and touch the bottom. It looks to be just below the surface."

Reaching into what probably was the purest pool of water they'd ever seen, Peter was clear up to his shoulder before he pulled out his dripping arm. "The bottom's not as close as it looks. This is the clearest water, Katie. I bet it tastes just divine." Cupping his hand, he helped himself to a mouthful. "Mmm," he groaned, closing his eyes. "I knew it. It's delicious."

Flinging the lantern down with reckless abandon, Katie cupped her hands as Peter had done and drank from the seemingly bottomless pool. "It's so crisp I just want to bite it," she squeaked, slurping at another mouthful.

Peter nodded. Tiny droplets of water dripped from his lips. "Me too."

Having drunk her fill, Katie sat back on the chilled ground. "And it's so cool in here." Tilting her head back, she let the chilled cave envelop her roasting body. "It actually makes this dress bearable!" Katie shivered, relishing the goose bumps that cropped up along her arms inside the dark, long sleeves.

Peter removed his hat and stared at her. Wordlessly, he reached down and helped her to her feet. "You're really very beautiful Katie." His voice was edged in such sincerity that Katie's knees wobbled. "That fire inside you—the same one that burns inside me and aches for adventure—makes me love you all the more." Setting his hat by the pool of water, Peter moved toward her.

Without thinking, Katie stretched out her hands and stepped to meet him. "Peter, I would like to tell you that—"

Gently, he laid a finger across her lips. "Hush, sweet Katie. Let's enjoy this adventure. We have the rest of our lives to say words to one another." Peter's breath was warm on her chilled face as he leaned in close.

Katie closed her eyes and stretched to the tips of her toes. *Could this be it? Our first real, shared kiss?*

"Well, what do we have here?" A cold voice came from the furthest recesses of the cave, resounding with an eerie echo. "Just who I was lookin' for."

Katie dropped back behind Peter, heart thundering in her chest. *Forgive me God, but I'm quite thankful for Peter's pistol right now.*

Footsteps clunked against the cave floor. "Who knew you liked to hide out with outlaws, too?"

Katie squinted into the darkness, but could make out nothing more than a sinister figure cloaked in darkness. Something rang with familiarity in the slightly nasal toned voice. "Jesse James took refuge here, so the legend goes. History books will confirm the fact that Johnny Tyler did, too."

Johnny Tyler! I knew it, Katie thought, her hands balling into fists.

His face more gaunt and wicked than before, Johnny staggered out of the shadows and into the pale light afforded by the lone lantern.

Chapter 6

Meramec Caverns
Outlaw Country, Missouri

“You people don't believe in carryin' guns, do ya?” Johnny fairly spat the words on the cave floor. “Guess there's no need to search ya.” Pulling a flask from his pocket, the young outlaw tilted back his head and treated himself to a long swill. Greasy clumps of black hair fell back over his shoulder. “So, what to do with you now?” Wiping his lip on his crusty sleeve, he took a step toward them.

“Go on back to the buggy, Katie. Get out of here,” Peter whispered. His voice was throaty and harsh. Never taking his eyes off Johnny, Peter made no motion to retrieve the knuckleduster from his pocket.

Katie's brow furrowed. “No, I am not leaving you,” she whispered back.

Johnny's maniacal laugh echoed off the damp walls of the cave, making icy fingers of fear claw their way up Katie's legs. “Won't do no good. While you two were off explorin' the cave, I took care of your horse and *buggy*.” His hate-filled words dripped with disdain.

“What did you do to Sookie?” Katie demanded, forgetting to be scared.

Johnny flung up his arms, sending a wave of whiskey cascading out behind him. “I just hobbled it, woman! What do you take me for," he slurred, "some sort of monster that would hurt a poor, defenseless Aim-ish buggy horse?" Johnny grinned, revealing a missing front tooth. "But don't you go gettin' no ideas now. You couldn't get that horse put back on that sad excuse for a wagon before I'd—" he held up his shooting iron and raised his voice sarcastically— "shot you in the back."

She wrinkled her nose. *Well, aren't you a coward.* Katie bit back the words before they flew off her tongue and got them both killed.

"Would take a real man to shoot an unarmed person in the back," Peter growled. "And a woman, at that."

Shifting his rotten, weepy gaze to Peter, Johnny's hand flew so fast that Katie barely had time to jump back as the pistol cut through the air. It found its mark on the side of Peter's head, sending her fearless protector first to his knees, then to the ground.

"Oops," Johnny mocked, his arms up as though he'd simply dropped a biscuit.

Stooping to Peter's side, Katie laid a hand on his neck. There was a strong pulse. "Peter, Peter, are you alright?" Her voice rose, threatening to break into a sob. With Peter's back to Johnny, he slowly opened one eye. And winked.

Understanding immediately and, for once thinking before she spoke, Katie pulled herself to her full height and squared her shoulders. "What do you want with us," she demanded. *I don't know what Peter is planning, but if he wants Johnny to think he's knocked out, then I will play along.*

"I want what I wanted before. You cheated me out of it." Johnny scratched his head with the shooting end of his pistol. "He humiliated me. Threw me in a horse trough, for Heaven's sake. And you…" His voice trailed off into the musical darkness. "You are now all mine."

Johnny stepped over Peter, his eyes burning like hot coals as he stared at her. A sadistic smile curled his lips upward in a broken, twisted grimace. "Come here, girl."

Katie took a step back. "No." *Though I walk through the valley of the shadow of death, I will fear no evil for Thou art with me…*

Johnny froze. A flash of anger contorted his features. "Yes." He began his approach again, but stumbled.

"No!" Turning on her heel, Katie dashed to the back of the cave, just outside the lantern's warm glow. *Let the darkness hide me, God. Help me, please.*

Johnny looked up, the drink having slowed his reflexes considerably. "Where you at, girl? You know I'm gonna find you."

From where Katie was hidden, behind a giant spike that rose from the floor, she could see everything. Johnny's stumbling attempt at following her was almost laughable as he tripped over his own foot yet again. Craning her neck, the person she didn't see was Peter.

He's hidden, too. Now just to stay quiet. So quiet. Katie sucked in a breath and willed her thundering heart to slow. *God, I don't know how to get out of this one. I know Peter doesn't want to kill a man, and I don't either. If there's another way, please show it.*

Johnny skulked around, obviously trying to decide which way to go. "Come here, girl," he sang. "Come on out now."

Katie sucked in her lower lip. Her heart had slowed a bit, but if not for the musical water dripping all about, she was sure Johnny could still track her to her hiding spot by how hard it was pounding. Something brushed her hand before coming to rest on top of it. *Peter, thank Go—*

Glancing at her hand, Katie was powerless to stop the shrill scream that tore from her throat at such a decibel, her entire tongue trembled. The thing that sat on her hand was huge, and neither fully spider nor fully scorpion. Long pinschers were folded before what was most likely its head, and legs of all sizes protruded from the sides. Long, whip-like antennae waved from the creature's back end up over its head, as though it was testing the air.

Springing up from her hiding place, Katie made no motion to stem her scream but shook her hand violently. "Get it off, get it off, get it off!" she shrieked, giving away her hiding place to any and every outlaw in the tri-county area.

That tell-tale wicked grin masked Johnny's face again. "Why Katie, there you are."

He didn't have time to step forward before a strange, foreign noise filled the air. Both Johnny and Katie looked up, but there was nothing to be seen but blackness. *Chirps? Beating wings? What is that?*

"Katie, duck!" Peter's voice boomed in the cave just before he tackled her to the floor. And not a moment too soon. "Don't move," he whispered.

Sure enough, the beating wings and flapping sounds grew in intensity and echoed off the cave walls. A sheet, blacker than the darkness of the cave, appeared from nowhere, flapping over their heads. Chirping and calling, thousands of bats beat their way free of the cavern in an unending, terrified wave, bringing the temperature of the cavern from cool to noticeably warmer.

"You woke the bats with your scream," Peter whispered into her ear in urgent tones. "See how they're headed for the entrance we squeezed through?"

"That explains the strange smell in here," Katie mused as she watched the flapping through one eye.

A shrill scream that rivaled hers tore from the depths of Johnny's very being as he made haste for the exit. "Bats in my hair! Bats in my shirt!" he screeched as the cranky bats unknowingly won the battle for Katie and Peter. "Help!"

In the excitement, Katie watched as his pistol was flung to the floor of the cave. "I'll get it," Katie whispered. Before Peter could stop her, she crawled from their hiding place on her belly beneath the pulsating throng of bats. She retrieved the gun just as Johnny squeezed through the exit and into the mouth of the cave.

Crawling back to the safety of their hiding place below the waning flock of bats, something hit her shoulder. When she reached Peter's side, she pushed herself into a sitting position. "Oh, what's this?"

"You picked up a rider," Peter said, leaning closer to her shoulder. Carefully, he examined the baby bat stuck to her dress.

Katie felt her facial features soften as she looked upon the tiny, big-eyed creature. "He's so tiny," she cooed.

Smiling, Peter gently unhooked the baby bat's claws from the dark fabric. "Let's let him go, shall we?" With a slight toss upward, the tiny bat took flight, squeaking, before catching up with the remaining winged creatures of the night.

Absently, Katie pulled Johnny's weapon from her dress pocket. "Here you go, Peter."

Peter accepted the weapon and tucked it into the waistband of his britches.

"He was so sweet," Katie gushed, still staring after the tiny bat. "Wish we could have kept him."

Peter rolled his eyes and helped Katie to her feet. "Well, you thwarted the outlaw. With the help of a thousand angry bats and one little pup. I think that's what baby bats are called. Anyhow," Peter shook his head and rubbed at the spot where the pistol had met his skull, "how about we check on that fire and get out of Missouri. I reckon they call it Outlaw Country for a reason."

Remembering the events that had just transpired, Katie suddenly balked, steeling her jaw. "Were you going to save me this time, Peter? I felt all alone."

Pausing, Peter swept Katie's hands up in his. "Sweet Katie, have a bit of faith. I was hiding behind a pointed rock, same as you. I had that knuckleduster trained on Johnny Tyler the entire time, praying for a way to get out of this mess without becoming a murderer." Those sea-green eyes glistened with intensity. "No matter what I had to do though, I wasn't going to let him lay one finger on the woman I love."

"I prayed the same prayer," Katie said softly. Her heart humbled at God's majesty.

"God sure provided, didn't He?" Peter's face broke into a brilliant grin. "Come on, let's go spread His love and glory all the way to Texas—He's worthy of it. Obviously, they aren't ready for either of us in Heaven just quite yet."

Hands clasped together in newfound admiration, Katie kept pace with Peter. As they squeezed through the opening and into the giant mouth of the cave, Katie was surprised to taste the fresh air. "Hey Peter, I think the fire went out."

"Fire stalled about a mile west of here." A familiar voice echoed off the sooty walls. A moment later, Bob Dalton stepped into view. "I apprehended a fellow that ran from this very cave. Hollerin' something about bats. He was trying desperately hard to get your horse hooked up to your distinctive buggy. At least, that's what he was doin' when I caught him." Bob grinned. "Hello again, Katie Knepp." Barely adjusting his seat, he offered an obligatory tip of his hat. "Peter."

Chapter 7

Missouri

“This is my last bounty, you know.” Bob drew a long drink from the steaming tin cup. They had thought it wise to build a small campfire ringed heavily in rocks. Surrounded by nothing to burn, there wasn't much chance of their meager campfire getting out of hand. Bob set his cup down. Katie refilled it at once with boiling coffee.

Bound, gagged, and still part drunk, Johnny slouched with his back turned, just at the edge of the fire's glow.

Peter spoke first. “Last one? Why's that Bob?”

Bob stared at Katie, a funny little smile on his lips. “What was that Peter?” he asked after a moment, his eyes still fixed on Katie. “Oh right, well, fact of the matter is, I said I'd be done after the Burrows boarded the train to justice.” Finally tearing his gaze from her, Bob retrieved the freshly refilled cup from beside the fire. “Many thanks, Miss Katie.”

Katie flushed from the direct attention as Bob drew another steaming sip off the top before continuing. “I was headed for Indian Territory to meet my brothers when I run smack into ole Johnny Tyler there.” Gesturing over to the sad excuse for a man, Bob grinned. “Reckon his bounty will pay me enough to at least get *started* out in Indian Territory.”

Peter nodded, but something soured in Katie's stomach. To speak of a man's life being worth the price of *getting started* didn't sit well with her. *Even if it is a creepy old goat like Johnny Tyler.* "What did he do to earn a bounty on his head?" The words on her tongue made her shudder.

"Things that are proper to speak of in polite comany," Bob answered. "I can't say for sure he's worth more dead than alive, but we'll soon see."

"So I reckon," Bob said, leaning back with this fingers laced behind his head. "I could see you folks on through to Springfield since I'm headed that way anyway. That is the next big town, you know." He licked his lips absently. "And since you two can't seem to steer clear of the outlaw element in this wild country, you could use me around for help."

Katie hid a smile and adjusted her covering. "We'd be honored, wouldn't we Peter."

From the other side of the campfire, Peter grunted.

"So, what made you fellows decide to take shelter in Robber's Roost?"

Katie cocked her head. "Robber's Roost?"

"That cave. A notorious hideout for the bandits of the area. Legend says the caves go all the way back to Canadee and down deep in the earth."

Katie adjusted her seat and stifled a yawn. "You certainly seem to know a lot about it, Mr. Dalton."

Bob flashed a smile that made her heartbeat quicken. She dropped her gaze from his. "Never know when I might have to take cover in there someday, Miss Katie. Seems there's a fine line in these wild parts, between the right side and the wrong side of the law."

Katie puzzled over his words for a moment. *Surely right is right and wrong is wrong, even out here?*

Bob's eyelids drooped. "Peter, would you mind sharing

watch with me again tonight? I'm happy to share the bounty money from Mr. Tyler with you."

Raising his steely stare, Peter nodded curtly. They'd come a long piece from Robber's Roost already, but the threat of fire still hung thick in the air. Judging by the burned spots, the fire appeared to have jumped and skipped all over the woods. Katie shivered as she looked at the rest of the drought-thirsty trees and bushes that would feed a roaring fire, should one erupt.

Peter's voice was gruff. "I'll help stand watch, for the outlaw *and* the fire. But I won't be needing any of the money that comes from it." Standing up suddenly, Peter glanced from Bob to Katie and then back to Bob. "I'll take first watch."

"You're the boss," Bob said through a yawn. The firelight accented his freckles, making him seem even more boyish and mischievous than before. Tilting his hat over his eyes, he was no doubt asleep before Katie even stood up.

"Thank you, Peter."

Wordlessly, Peter handed her a blanket from the wagon before disappearing into the woods.

No sooner had Katie closed her eyes than the voice was there, invading her foggy, weighted dreams. "Get up Katie. Run!" A hard yank on her arm brought her fully awake. Opening her eyes, they immediately burned from the thick, pungent smoke.

Arms plucked her up and flung her into the buggy. Her voice sounded strange and foreign to her own ears, and her words came out in a screech. "What's happening?"

"Hot spot flared up, as I figure it."

Bob was on his horse bareback, with the bound and gagged outlaw flung over the flank like a sack of potatoes. Awkwardly, the young bounty hunter held his horse's reins with one hand and the squirming outlaw Johnny Tyler with the other. "We're gonna have to make a run for it," he shouted over the din of the roaring inferno. "Fire's got us surrounded!"

Katie glanced wildly around the campsite. *Was this my fault? Did I put out the campfire?* Remembering her actions over the course of the night, she exhaled when the realization came into focus in her sleep-heavy mind. *It wasn't my fault. I drowned the campfire in dirt.*

"Surrounded?" Peter called back. "Not possible, Bob."

Glancing around wildly, Katie's stomach soured as she watched the animals that wouldn't normally have been seen together in the wild take refuge behind each other in their modest camp. Skunks and a mountain lion. Foxes and a small black bear. Mice of all sorts and even a handful of snakes, the likes of which Katie had never seen before. A singed coyote took shelter behind a very nervous Sookie. Katie gulped.

Johnny Tyler had somehow managed to loosen his gag. "It's my boys! They're gonna set me free by fire," he hollered, his voice maniacal. "They set this fire, you fools!"

"Oh shut up," Bob shouted back, giving him a shake. "You work alone, you big lug. Everybody knows that."

Peter snapped the reins over Sookie's back. "Let's go!" Raring, the black mare dashed ahead. Katie could make out Bob's voice back behind them somewhere, calling and yelling, but she couldn't quite piece together the words. Just as the ravenous orange flames came into sight, Sookie stopped. Flinging her large black head, she dug in her hooves and refused to move any further toward the roaring inferno.

Shoving the reins into Katie's sweaty palms, Peter had to shout to be heard. "Here, drive." Bounding off the seat, he ripped off his shirt in one fluid motion. "She's spooked at the wildfire!"

Despite the adrenaline that surged through her veins, Katie looked at Peter, at Sookie, then back at Peter. Her eyes widened as she took in the sight of his chiseled back and arms. Farm work had sculpted every muscle to perfection and, as he flung his shirt over Sookie's eyes, Katie was powerless to stop her eyes from roaming over the man who could have been her husband by now, if not for this harebrained Texas journey idea.

Forgive those thoughts, God, Katie prayed. Then, laughing at the inappropriateness of the entire situation, she tried to focus her attention on driving the buggy.

Suddenly, everything jerked beneath her. *We're going through the fire?* As absurd as it was, Katie had simply been willing to ride beside Peter wherever he saw fit to take her. However now that she was alone in the buggy, everything seemed wrong. An ocean of fear swirled over her as the fire roared and crackled all around. Squeezing her eyes shut as tightly as she could manage, Katie bit her tongue so she wouldn't scream.

The stifling heat threatened to melt her skin, her hair, her everything as they drove through the dancing flame. Too scared to call out for fear of sucking in the suffocating fire, Katie's mind clung to Peter. No matter how much she hurt on the buggy seat, he was more exposed than she. *Please God, let him be alright. Let my Peter be alright. Let us all be alright...*

Almost as quickly as it began, it was over. The intense burning was gone and the coolness of the night's air kissed her sizzling skin. *Thank you, God. We made it through!* Flinging off her singed covering, she called out in a raspy voice. "Peter?"

Silence, set against the backdrop of the retreating fire, met her ears.

Hopping out of the buggy, Katie saw that Sookie had made it, too. "Oh Sookie, where's Peter?" she cried, dashing to the heaving side of the faithful mare. "I have to tell him—"

"Tell him what?" asked a voice from the other side of the skittish black horse.

Bending, Katie found Peter. *Thank you, God.* Squatted down, he was busily tending the burns on Sookie's ankles. He'd already pulled what was left of his shirt, the light blue one she'd made him, into strips and was tying it around the raw-looking injuries. Surprisingly, Sookie was letting him.

"She never has let anyone touch her feet, has she," Katie murmured, almost in passing.

Peter brushed his forearm across his brow. "No, she's always been notoriously hostile when it comes to her hooves."

Katie rubbed her hands over Sookie's singed coat, pinching out any glowing orange ends of horsehair. Cooing softly, Sookie seemed to understand that everything was going to be alright now.

Peter stood and patted Sookie gently on the rump. "I told you I couldn't let anything happen to the woman I love." With a wink that bespoke of a secret shared just between the two of them, he disappeared behind the mare again.

"Peter, I have to tell you that I—"

"Shush Katie. Nothing like that until after the journey's over, alright?" Peter knotted the last bandage and stood up.

Katie stood motionless, powerless to stop her eyes from

roving over the shapely, exposed torso of the man who'd saved her life. Again.

"Well, she's finally at a loss for words," Peter joked.

Katie furrowed her brow. "Peter, how did we make it through that fire without burning up? It felt like my skin was melting right off. And if I was burning on the inside of the buggy, you on the outside had to be—" Her words trailed off into the night.

"So what you're asking is, how come I'm not burnt to a crisp?" His lips teased upward into a flirty smile.

Katie, however, was in no mood to flirt. "Was it a miracle, Peter? Did God see us through that fire?"

Peter shrugged. "Of course. His hand has been on everything we've encountered this trip. But as for how we got through, I saw a break in the flames."

Katie exhaled the breath she didn't know she had been holding.

"He is watching over us, Katie. No doubt about it. That break—" Peter gestured toward the burnt blackness. "There was no reason in the world it should have been there. God gave us a path, but left it up to us to find."

Before she could open her mouth to answer, Bob galloped up. His blue eyes, no longer dancing, were wide. "Did you see him? Did he come this way?"

"Who?" Katie asked. Her eyes flickered to the rump of his horse, which was now empty. Icy fingers of dread squeezed her throat. "Where's Johnny?" she squeaked.

Bob's voice came out too high-pitched to be normal. "That sapsucker wasn't lyin'! He *does* have boys, and they *did* set that fire." He glanced wildly from Peter to Katie. "They runned right up and snatched him off my horse! Gave 'er a swat and sent me into the flames."

Peter's voice was strong, like a wise, old, gnarled oak. "We'd better put as much distance between them and us as possible then." Walking around Sookie, Peter offered his arm to Katie. After helping her into the buggy, he spoke again. "Johnny knew which way we were headed, didn't he, since it was all the talk around the campfire just a few hours ago."

Bob hung his head, the weight of his possibly deadly error hanging thick in the air.

"We were headed to Springfield. I say the safest bet is to keep on that way."

Bob looked up. "But they may be waiting up ahead to ambush us."

Peter snapped the reins and Sookie, still a bit skittish, started off at a spooky trot. Bob kept up beside them, glancing over first one shoulder, then the other.

"Johnny Tyler's a coward," Peter attested. "I've bested him once; Katie's bested him once. He knows you want the money on his head. He'll go the direct opposite way from us, I reckon."

Katie scooted closer to her protector.

"We'll go until we reach water or a town, and there we will make camp. We could all use a rest." He flashed another knowing grin to Katie. Her stomach immediately turned up in knots. *Oh, Peter let me tell you that I love you.*

"Sounds like a plan," Bob called, glancing over his shoulder again. "Certainly would feel safer if I hadn't lost my gun back there somewhere."

Peter ignored him and stared softly at Katie. "Your hair looks beautiful falling around your shoulders like that, Katie girl."

She wound her hands together in her lap, at a loss for words for the second time that day.

Delighting in her sudden shyness, Peter nudged her with his elbow. "What possessed you to take off your covering?"

"It was full of holes from the fire burning through," she stammered. Content to keep her mouth shut, she stared straight ahead. Still though, she admired Peter through new eyes by way of frequent sideways glances.

"Looks to be as good a place as any to camp," Bob called from behind them. The lights of Springfield glittered just up ahead under the dark sky.

"Why not just get a hotel room in Springfield?" Katie's voice dropped with sleep.

Peter pushed a lock of chestnut-colored hair back behind her ear. "That costs cash money, and I'm assuming Mr. Dalton has about as much as we do, now. Which isn't much." He reined Sookie to a stop. "Looks good to me too, Bob," Peter agreed. Still, the sly little smile appeared on his lips whenever he caught Katie's glance, which was often. A shared secret alright. A shared secret of love.

"I'll take first shift this time," Bob offered. "Last time you went on watch, we got caught in a forest fire." The younger man offered a familiar nod to Peter, who laughed.

"That is true."

Bob helped Katie pull a ratty quilt from the back of the buggy. Miraculously, it has managed to survive the fire, along with another of his shirts and the rest of the goods they'd packed. "I'll wake you in an hour. Katie, you rest assured Ole Bob ain't gonna let nothing get us."

Ignoring him, Katie spread out the quilt for Peter and offered him his fresh shirt before producing another quilt for herself.

"You take the buggy seat, Katie," Peter whispered as he accepted the articles. As he took them, their hands brushed. Peter let his linger there, his skin touching hers, a moment before flinging the quilt about his shoulders.

"Okay," Katie whispered, losing herself for a moment in the touch. Peter tucked her in tightly on the buggy seat. With another heart-stopping wink, he retreated to his own pallet by the wobbly front wheel. Covering himself with the quilt, he tucked the fresh shirt under his head for a pillow. Before Katie could start a prayer of gratitude and thanks, sleep turned her eyelids to stone.

Katie dipped her feet in the river, letting the icy water swirl over her toes and splash against her ankles. She was supposed to be milking the cow, but the barn was stifling in the muggy summer heat and the river proved to be much too inviting.

"Sister," Annie admonished from behind her. "How could you sneak off to our spot and not invite me along?" Kicking off her black shoes, Annie rushed to join her.

Katie grinned and hugged her sister. "You were churning butter and I know how much you hate to be interrupted."

Annie rolled her eyes. "I love the river more." Her sister, as beautiful on the outside as she was on the inside, glanced over her shoulder. "Uh oh, we're caught. Here comes Ma."

"Katie," Katherine Knepp called from across the meadow. "Katie .... Katie... Katie..."

Someone shook her shoulder. "Katie, hey Katie. Wake up." Opening her eyes, the lovely dream fizzled and left her heart heavy. Her mother's musical voice turned into that of Bob Dalton. Katie scowled. "What is it?"

"Sun's almost up. Katie, I have to talk to you." Bob squatted on his heels and rubbed his hands together. He was fully dressed for the day, as though he'd been awake for some time, and looked rather anxious.

Katie rubbed the sleep from her eyes and sat up, struggling to make her world not only come into focus, but for it to make sense as well. "You leaving, Bob?"

"Oh Katie," he said, looking at her more intently than she felt was necessary. The horrible taste in her mouth made her cover her face with her hand before she spoke.

"What, Bob?"

The young bounty hunter smiled. "You remind me of everything pure and good in this world Katie Knepp—heck, you *are* everything pure and good."

Katie listened to his whispers, not comprehending.

"I've been watching you sleep."

Uneasiness quaked in her stomach beneath his intense stare.

"You're everything I'm not, Katie. You're also everything I want out of life."

Katie stole a glance at Peter, sleeping soundly under the same quilt his mother gave him the day he came to live with the Amish.

"Come with me, Katie. Let Peter go on with his life. Come with me and let's live a life of adventure. Live it out together."

She hesitated, shifting her weight on the seat. "Bob, I—"

Obviously sensing her impending refusal, he reached forward and clasped her hands in his. Bob Dalton's blue eyes were wide as he searched her face. "Me and my brothers can track down the bandits with our security firm and you can save their souls with that quiet, gentle way of yours." He looked pointedly toward the horizon. It was just beginning to turn a hazy gray. "Let's go, Katie. The time is now. Come with me. Marry me."

"A life of adventure," she began carefully, "is something I already have planned with Peter."

Bob's face registered disappointment, but only for a moment. "Can you honestly tell me you love him and not me?"

Katie nodded.

His hard-lined mouth softened into a defeated smile as Bob lifted Katie's hands to his lips. "Can't blame a feller for tryin'. Good luck in Texas, Katie Knepp." Brushing the tops of her hands with a dry kiss, Bob tipped his hat again. Silent, he swung onto the back of his horse and disappeared into the fast encroaching dawn.

Stepping from her nest in the buggy, Katie walked to the edge of camp. Her arms hugged tightly to her chest to guard against the morning's chill; she watched him go until he was a just a far-off speck. "Goodbye, Bob Dalton. May God go with you," she whispered.

Turning back toward camp, she walked back to where Peter lay sleeping. *I could have gone with Bob and Peter wouldn't have known for hours*, she thought. She watched as Peter's back moved with each of his deep, rhythmic breaths. Glancing at the horizon, Bob's figure was gone. *Who could have even considered such a thing?*

Carefully so as not to wake him, Katie lay down next to Peter. Propping her head upon her hand, she snaked her other arm across his still bare chest and squeezed lightly. "Since you are asleep, I expect my saying this doesn't count. But I have to say it. I love you, Peter. I always have, even through my most stubborn moments, I have loved you. I know God made my match when He made you. I love you." She moved her face closer until her lips brushed his skin. "I love you, Peter. I *love* you! I will marry you. Someday."

Before she could even hope for a response from her sleeping beau, a bobcat dashed into camp. "Well, good morning cat," Katie said, shocked at the feline's bold entrance.

At the sound of her voice, the bobcat jerked its fluffy head toward her, as though noticing her for the first time.

"Good morning," she said again, studying the small wild animal. Something about it didn't look quite right. In the eyes, it looked everywhere but at her. It seemed jittery, on edge, and long strands of drool slimed at the corners of its mouth.

"Good morning," Peter said, turning over heavily. "What have we here?"

"A bobcat."

Peter's sleepy smile sobered. "A bobcat?"

Katie nodded toward the animal that just stood there, staring at the pair of them.

Peter rose slowly. "I take that to mean it's time to go. Here, let me help you into the buggy."

The cat simply stood, staring at them as they clambered into the buggy. Carefully, as though it were sporting a righteous headache, the cat started after them. When they slowed, it slowed. When they sped up, the bobcat sped up. "Isn't that strange," Katie mused, craning her neck out the buggy's window.

Peter nodded as he drove Sookie down the Missouri trail.

Funny, Katie thought as they rode along in comfortable silence. *Peter didn't even ask about Bob.* She opened her mouth to make mention of his leaving but closed it again on second thought.

Chapter 8

Vinita, Indian Territory

"**I**s it because of the fire?"

Peter glanced at her, still wearing the mysterious smile. He'd slid his fresh shirt on before they'd left camp, but the day had already grown so warm, that he'd rolled the sleeves partway up his arm. "Is what because of the fire?"

She gestured over her shoulder. "The bobcat. It's still following us."

"Really?" Peter glanced out his window. He sighed and snapped the reins. "I don't think so, Katie."

Katie sucked in her bottom lip. It was already well past midday and the little cat still followed them. Never did she feel threatened but instead she sensed, on some level, that the little bobcat simply wanted to be near them. "Doesn't it make sense that if an animal is threatened by fire it will act strangely?"

"Yes, that makes sense, but I don't see any other animals acting like this. Something about this particular animal just doesn't feel right."

Katie contemplated their situation for a moment. "I think it just likes us, Peter," she reasoned. "Maybe if you pull over, I can pet it."

Peter looked at her as though she'd just recited the Gettysburg Address in Latin. "No Katie, that cat's sick. See how Sookie's acting?" It was true. Their buggy horse had kept up a steady trot all day, despite her singed ankles. "See, she senses that we're getting close to town and is pouring on the steam."

"She's doing what?"

Peter smiled. "Going faster."

Katie shrugged. "Oh," she said, pointing to a sign. "Va-nee-tah." She glanced at Peter for approval. "Vinita?"

"That's what it looks like to me." He shifted on the seat. "Welcome to Indian Territory, my dear Katie girl."

Katie's eyes widened as they pulled into Vinita. "So this is what Indian Territory looks like," she whispered, awe softening her words.

"Let's park the buggy at the livery and see what we can get to eat." Peter climbed down and reached to assist Katie.

Once in the street, Katie's hands flew to her exposed hair. "Oh Peter, I can't be seen without my covering, and—" Her worried face melted into one of indignation. "Hold on there now. I thought you said that we were fresh out of cash money."

Peter gave her hand a squeeze and winked. "I may have had enough to take care of us. But Bob Dalton? He can take care of himself."

Katie arched an eyebrow in spite of herself. "What do I do for a covering?"

Peter crossed his arms and glanced up and down the wooden boardwalks that lined both sides of the street. She did the same. Though a bit tumbledown, the settlement of Vinita looked a smidge closer to how she had been picturing Old Amarillo to look.

"Ah, there now," Peter said, pointing to one of the brightly painted building façades. "Can you read that word on there, Katie?"

Katie stared at the word, trying the letters out on her

tongue before trusting herself enough to try them aloud. She'd never been a star pupil and had focused more on causing grief for the smarter kids, like Rebekah Stoll, than applying herself to her studies. Her Pa had told her once that she had done just fine, reading the letters she thought she saw, but they were the wrong ones for the word. Truth be told, the letters tended to jump around and flip upside down when she concentrated on them too much, making anything she said come out wrong.

It had only taken once when the entire one-roomed schoolhouse in Gasthof Settlement let a soft snicker pass over them while Katie was reading aloud from the blackboard. Never again had she even bothered to attempt a public reading. At least, not until Peter asked her to.

"Mer," Katie started. "Merchant's Tile?"

Peter nodded. "Close. Mercantile. That's where you're going to pick out your fabric for a new covering."

Katie's face, hangdog at her mispronunciation of the word, brightened. She pulled back her shoulders. "Really, Peter?"

"Really, Katie. But there's only one condition."

Katie's resolve threatened to falter. "Oh?"

"Pick out both a white fabric and a black fabric." Peter flashed a grin. "That way, if you ever consent to marry me, your black wedding covering will be all ready."

Biting back her tongue, Katie had to physically cross her feet so as not to dash into his arms. Arms that looked so empty without her in them. Arms that were divinely made for her.

"That sounds good to me, Peter Wagler." Ducking her head, Katie hid her smile. *I can't wait to tell him that I love him. God grant me the patience that Peter requires of me now.*

"Better late than never," Peter chuckled, pointing down the road.

Sure enough, the bobcat had followed them into town.

As they watched the haphazard cat trot down the main street of Vinita, Katie called attention to the drool sliming from the cats frothy mouth, all the way down to the dusty road. "It's growling Peter," she said, stepping back behind her beau. Now, something about the unfortunate little cat made her want to run, hide and forget she ever saw it. *How foolish was I to want to pet it?*

From out of the saloon across the street, a lanky stranger staggered out to meet the day. Obviously hung over, he shielded his eyes from the sun as he stared at the buggy. A tiny smile came to his unshaven face and for a moment, Katie thought he might come over and speak to them. However, the out-of-place bobcat caught his attention first. His shooting iron was drawn from his holster in a flash and before Katie could suck in breath enough to offer any protest, the little bobcat was lying dead in the dusty road.

Fire flashed inside her where moments before, friendship could have bloomed. Just as she suspected earlier, the stranger strode over to make their acquaintance. Pistol holstered, the gunman's face was untelling of anything out of the ordinary. If one had just happened upon the scene, they never would have guessed the tall, smiling man had just gunned down a helpless bobcat. Katie's words flew off her tongue with a righteous air. "Just what do you think you're doing there, mister?"

Peter placed his hand lightly on her arm. "Katie."

"Is this the kind of place where a man can just shoot animals and that's that?"

"Katie." Peter's voice was more insistent as passersby were beginning to stop and take notice.

Flinging her hands into the air, Katie managed to tangle her fingers in her chestnut mane. "I'm starting to wonder if I shouldn't have just stayed in Gasthof."

"Katie!"

With a huff, Katie turned to face Peter. "What is it, Peter?" Tugging hard, she freed the last of her fingers from her tresses.

The pistol-packing stranger stood there in the street, grinning at her as though she'd just showed him a side of life he'd never seen. As opposed to entering into argument with Katie, he simply drew a flask from his vest pocket and tipped it to Peter. "Got your own little rabid cat there, don't ya, mister." He tipped up the flask and took a healthy swig. "Clayton Allison, at your service."

Peter stuck out his hand. "Mr. Allison, hallo. Thank you for the fine welcome." He glanced at Katie. "And for dispatching that rabid bobcat before any harm could come to us or anyone else in the fine town of Vinita."

Clayton nodded, the smile fading from his shadowed face. Strikingly handsome, Katie let her eyes roam over the raven haired gunman. The severe part in his shining locks gave the impression of waves curling back from over his spring-time-green eyes. *Or are they blue?* Katie leaned in closer to get a better look. *Maybe they're a bit of both, yes that's it. A bit of both, like the ocean.* A frazzled tuft of curls had apparently lost their pomade and poked out at the peak of his forehead.

"Sorry, I'm not better company today, folks. Fact of the matter is, I just plunged you, me, and this whole God-for-sake—" He paused in his spiel and glanced at Katie. "Excuse me there, ma'am. This whole part of the country into progress."

Clayton wrinkled his nose and stuck his tongue out the corner of the mouth, as though he were trying to rid himself of a bad taste. "Progress. Ha! Progress for who—er, whom—is what I want to know."

Producing his flask again, Clayton helped himself to a hearty swig and ignored the indignant stares from the respectable townsfolk who congregated on the boardwalk. *Interesting how those folks never step off into the red dirt street.* Katie was intrigued by the man who was probably only a decade or so older than she herself was.

"I'm sorry Mr. Allison, but how did you fling us into progress?" Clayton's eyes twinkled, bemused, as he looked at Katie. "Ah, the wide-eyed face of innocence." He jutted his jaw and stared off over the tops of the buildings, into the wild blue sky. "I'll tell you darlin', I flung this here part of the world into progress because earlier this week I singlehandedly escorted the last of the wild Comanche chiefs to an Army base just a ways south of here." He blinked back moisture and his lower lip quivered. "It was there, at a place called Fort Sill, where Chief Quanah Parker surrendered his freedom to the Great White Father."

Katie tried to follow along, but the words Mr. Allison chose to use served more to confound her than anything else. "You can probably tell we're new to your part of the country," Katie said quietly. "I don't know anything about a Quanah Parker, or a Great Father in White." As much as she willed it not to, as much as she just simply wanted to move on down the trail with Peter to their long-awaited home in Texas, Katie's heart began to pound. This was an adventure she had to hear.

"Is that so? Well, I'll tell you this. There was a time when the Comanche Indians, or as they called themselves—The People —roamed free. Then the white people started moving into their land and generally making a nuisance of themselves." Clayton spoke with such a knowledgeable tongue that Katie was intrigued. She recognized the passion right off, too. Her lack of a covering momentarily forgotten, she leaned farther forward to absorb as much of the story as she could from Mr. Allison's lips.

"As you can probably imagine, wars began. Land wars, people wars, these wars, those wars—all us Texans knew what was going to happen, where it all was leading." Clayton sighed deeply. "Then the day came that too many Indians had died. Too many whites, too. And, of course, when you're dealing with the government, too much money had been lost."

English people certainly talk more about money than anything else.

Clayton wobbled a bit but caught himself on the side of the buggy before he fell completely to the ground. "It was time for the Comanche to surrender, or the Army was going to wipe 'em all off the faith—er, excuse me, face—of the earth." Clayton burped into his fist before continuing. "Quanah Parker, the great chief that he is, decided to do what was best for his tribe and surrender. And I was the unlucky son-of-a-buck who got to take his freedom away." A tear leaked from the corner of Clayton's eye. Without trying to appear as though she was staring, Katie adjusted herself to get a better look. *Yup, indeed. This gunfighter is crying.*

Clayton Allison sniffled back the rest of his tears before drawing another long gulp from his flask. "So I escorted Chief Parker from his home range in Texas, which was quite near my ranch mind you, right up to the gate at Fort Sill.

Wouldn't go in myself though, no sir. I got my principles you see." Clayton patted the buggy and stepped back a ways to test out his balance. "Once I done that, I just kept on a-comin' north. Time to forget the whole business. I mean shoot," he went on, gesturing wildly with one arm. "I could almost hear those ranchers banging up the barbed wire fences behind us as we left Texas." He stumbled back over and leaned nonchalantly against the buggy, squinting, even though, his back was to the sun. "Little lady, you're lookin' at the durn fool who tamed the West that day." Clayton ducked his head and sniffled back another round of tears.

Never having met his equal, Katie glanced at Peter, who shrugged and commenced to examining his fingernails.

Katie stepped a bit nearer to Clayton. "You're from Texas then?"

"Yes, ma'am. Down around San Antone."

Nodding, Katie continued. "How blessed you were to have Mr. Parker, er Chief Parker, as your neighbor then."

Clayton sniffled again. "Well, we weren't rightly neighbors. Comanche range was further west. But you see," Clayton raised his head and pointed off to the south, "everyone in Texas is your neighbor. You'll see." He turned his back to the buggy and propped one leg up as though he were resting against his own wagon.

Turning, Katie mimicked his stance best she could. "Parker. Do all Indians have such English sounding names?"

A spark lit up Clayton's eyes, and he spun to face her, almost falling in the process. "You mean to tell me you've never heard the story of Cynthia Ann Parker? The white woman who was captured by the Comanche as a small girl, only to grow up and become a wife to a chief and mother to a future chief?"

Katie's jaw went slack. So much information spewed forth in Clayton's few words that taking it all in was like a water-logged garden being graciously sprinkled with more and more rain. "Texas certainly sounds, well, interesting." Katie forced a smile. Fact was; her mind was already out of Indian country and over the Red River, where all the excitement seemed to be.

"That sun's mighty hot. Would you two care to join me in the saloon for a drink?" He winked at Katie. "They offer sarsaparilla too, you know."

Sarsaparilla? That sounds fun—Katie opened her mouth to accept, but Peter cut her off. "No thanks, Mr. Allison. But we certainly thank you for your company."

"And for the stories," Katie chimed. She patted Peter's arm as Clayton Allison sauntered back into the saloon. "Texas is getting more interesting the closer we get."

Peter nodded, unimpressed. "Let's go pick you up that fabric. Those coverings aren't going to make themselves."

Katie was secretly glad Peter had insisted they bunk overnight at the hotel across from the saloon in Vinita. With Peter safely tucked into the room next to hers, Katie had the cloth for both coverings spread out across the small bed in the corner of her room. She sat at the roughshod desk by the window and stitched by candlelight to the tune of the plunky piano music coming from the saloon across the street.

The candle had almost burned down to a nub when a sudden fracas in the street called Katie's attention away from the nearly-finished coverings. She poked the needle into the fabric before jumping to her feet and hurrying to the window. With her nose pressed to the dirty glass, she could just make out the figures of two men tossing something back and forth to one another. "Hey, that's Clayton," Katie mused to her absent audience. Leaning to the wall that separated her room from Peter's, Katie gave the wall a bang. "Peter! Are you seeing this?"

Peter knocked back quietly. "Yes, Katie," he replied in a voice notably softer than the one she'd used. "You don't have to yell."

The corners of her mouth twitched upward. "Oh, you're right. Sorry." She thought she heard Peter's musical laugh from the other side of the thin wall.

A gunshot, not unlike the one that had taken the life of the sick bobcat earlier, rang out in the street below. "Oh my," she exclaimed, exhaling onto the glass. Rubbing furiously, so as to get a better look at the goings on outside, Katie let go a huff. *Most of the dirt is on the outside of the window.* By the time Katie got enough of the window cleaned off to peer out with more detail, everyone had already cleared away. Was Clayton part of that shootout?

Katie's shoulders sagged, and with a defeated sigh she blew a tuft of her russet bangs off her forehead. *I think Peter should go investigate.* She gave another soft knock to the wall. "Peter?"

No answer.

"Peter!" She knocked again, a bit louder. "Peter, are you awake?"

A dull thunk sounded from Peter's side of the wall. "I am now. What is it, Katie?"

She could hear the sleep still heavy in his voice. "Don't you think you should go out there and see what happened?"

Peter must have leaned against the wall because it pushed

in against her a little. "No. I don't think that would be a very smart thing to do."

Her mouth fell open. "Well," she stammered, "why not? Don't you want to know what happened?"

"You, I, and the entire settlement of Vinita heard what happened. There was a shot."

Katie peeked out the window again into the dark, quiet street. Though the lights of the saloon still burned bright, there was no more plunky piano music on out-of-tune keys echoing through the night. It looked as though all the saloon-goers had simply vanished. "What if Mr. Allison was involved? I am almost sure it was him in the street, tossing something with another man."

Peter sighed loudly. "Katie, don't you think that Mr. Allison knows how to handle a pistol?" He paused a moment. Whether he was giving her time to ponder his words or if he had dozed off, Katie wasn't sure. "He was quite drunk when we met him this afternoon, and still he managed to shoot a moving bobcat and kill it with one shot."

"Oh. I suppose you're right." Katie ran her fingers over a lock of her exposed hair. She examined the color and held it up to the wooden wall, comparing the tones. "You're right as usual."

There was a long silence. She could hear him shifting his weight on the creaky floorboards on his side of the wall. "Katie?"

"Yes?"

"Was there anything else?"

Katie thought for a moment. *Yes, there is something else. I want to come to your room and see if your window is any easier to see out of.* The question burned on her tongue, but she didn't ask it. "No, that's all."

"Okay. Goodnight, Katie. Sleep well."

Her voice was meek. "Goodnight." She listened as he climbed back into his bed. A moment later, she could hear his deep, rhythmic breathing. Retreating from the wall, Katie stole another glance outside. Still, there was nothing notable going on that she could see.

Picking up her covering, she pricked her finger on the needle. Not tired enough to sleep, she kept one eye on her sewing and one eye on the window.

Katie was up with the sun, partially because her hotel room faced east, and there were no curtains to block out the bright rays. Still, waking and greeting the day without daily chores was something she hadn't gotten entirely used to. Having fallen asleep watching the window, she plucked up the black covering and had just finished when a soft knock came at her door.

"Good morning Peter," she called gaily. *Only Peter can knock that softly.* Flinging open the door, Katie was pleased to discover Peter there, with matching plates of breakfast.

"Did the fabric work for your coverings, Katie?" His voice was subdued.

Of course, he doesn't want to wake up the English patrons who like to sleep late into the morning. "They did, thank you." Twisting her hair into a tight bun, she pulled on her new soft white covering. Of course, a handful of locks escaped. She tucked the stubborn locks back up where they belonged, only to have them fall back down again.

"Here, let me." Setting the plates on the night stand, Peter's fingers gently brushed her neck as he tucked her hair into place. "Beautiful," he breathed.

Goosebumps crept up Katie's arms. "I'm, um, packed. Ready to head for Texas?" Turning to face Peter, she tried to look comfortable in her skin. "Let's continue our adventure together." *I love you, Peter.*

Katie was just about to step into the buggy when a slumped figure from the side of the saloon caught her attention. She recognized the severe part and tuft of bangs in an instant. "Excuse me, Mr. Allison?" She took care to keep her voice low as she approached him. Squatting down in the mud, she could hear his muffled sobs. "What's wrong?"

"Hi, Katie darlin'. They won't put me in jail."

Katie looked hard at Clayton. "What did you say, Mr. Allison?"

"Sheriff won't put me in jail. I killed a man last night, and I even walked into the cell myself, but fool that he is he wouldn't lock the cell door."

Katie sucked in her bottom lip as the town of Vinita slowly came to life around them. "Well, forgive me for asking, but..." Katie let her voice trail off before she asked a question she might not have wanted to know the answer to. Giving over to her curiosity, she continued. "Why did you kill him?"

Clayton stretched out his legs in front of him and hung his head. "He called me an Indian Lover and drew down on me. I agreed with him and told him I wished I hadn't brought the Comanche in to surrender." He looked up from the mud, depressed and seemingly helpless. As well as hopelessly drunk. "Then I handed him one of my guns to kill me with."

Not knowing how to respond, Katie stared at Clayton before shifting her body and motioning for Peter to join her.

"By this time we were in the street," he continued. "Durn dude, he threw my pistol back at me! The durn thing discharged. Killed him dead. Now the ole sheriff is sayin' self-defense." Clayton pinched the bridge of his nose in such a way that a passerby would think the weight of the world rested on the young man's shoulders.

Katie glanced back at Peter. Sure enough, he was unsuccessfully hiding the smile that flickered on his lips like a candle flame.

"Well, I have never heard of such a thing," Peter said. "And I'm sorry Mr. Allison, but I have to agree with the sheriff. It sounds like you're innocent."

"He is innocent," a strong-featured man proclaimed as he marched up, fully sober, from the red dirt street. With a sincere smile, he offered his hand to first Katie, then Peter. "Howdy folks, I'm Bill White. This here's John Threepersons." He motioned behind him to a tall, lanky man, dark-skinned, with a flat top hat.

Katie nodded. "Hello, Bill. John."

Peter nodded at the men, an amused twinkle overtaking his eyes.

Leaning together as though choreographed, the men pulled Clayton out of the mud and hauled him to the horse trough that sat in front of the saloon.

"Ma'am, you may want to avert your eyes for this," John Threepersons warned. Then, he and Bill White proceeded to shove Clayton's head under the slimy, brackish water.

Katie gasped and looked at Peter. "Should we do something?"

Peter watched as the two men yanked their friend up by his collar. "Sober yet, Clay?" Bill called.

Clayton shook his head and babbled something about just going on and drowning him. "Again," the mystery friends agreed before dunking him back under water.

From behind his hand, Peter spoke Pennsylvania Dutch. "I don't think there's anything we can do that these men haven't already thought of, Katie."

Clayton's voice rang out, watery and loud. "I'm sober now you yellow-bellied sapsuckers!"

John Threepersons grinned, revealing one missing front tooth. "I declare you sober."

Clayton shook the horse spit out of his hair over the dusty road. "Forgive the theatrics Peter, Katie." Gesturing, he asked, "Have you fellows met Peter Wagler and Katie Knepp?"

Stone drunk and upset and he still remembered both our names?

"We met, Clay," Bill assured him. "Saloon keeper told us you were out here having a good cry 'cause the sheriff wouldn't arrest you." He shot a pained look to Katie. "John and I hurried over to see if there was anything we could do."

Something tells me this isn't the first time these two men have come to Mr. Allison's rescue.

Clayton tilted his chin skyward, a proud grin on his unshaven face. "No sir, I already done it."

Bill and John exchange a look. "What'd you already do, Clay?"

Straightening his vest, Clayton began to explain. "Well, when the good sheriff wouldn't keep me in jail, I paid a visit to the widow."

Katie licked her lips. "What widow?"

"The wife of the man I killed last night."

Bill sighed. "You didn't kill him, Clay. It was a fool accident. Everybody says so."

"Anyway, I paid her a visit. I apologized, and I gave her my ranch."

Bill and John shook their heads in unison. *They've obviously been friends with Mr. Allison for quite some time.* Katie followed Peter's lead and attempted to hide her smile behind her hand.

"It was the right thing to do," Clayton attested. Producing a comb from the pocket of his vest, he proceeded to groom himself in the saloon's front window.

Bill closed his eyes. "Oh, Clay. Please say you didn't."

He turned his head, checking his reflection from every angle. "All 10,000 acres of the Rockin' R, down San Antone way. And all the cowboys to work it now belong to the widow of—" Clayton stopped combing as a look of absolute horror overtook his face. "Boys, I don't even know the feller's name I kilt."

Bill and John exchanged a knowing look.

Replacing the comb, Mr. Allison resembled a banker more so than a gunfighter. Or a murderer. Or even a drunk. "I killed her husband, Bill; it was the least I could do."

"Did you marry up with her too?" John asked. From his tone, Katie couldn't tell if he was kidding or not.

"No, I'm already married boys, you know that." Clayton's eyes glassed over. "Excuse me fellas, Miss Knepp, but I have to go."

Bill flung his hands up. "Where you headed to now, Clay?"

Hurrying down the dusty street with his six guns still strapped to his hips, Clayton Allison offered only a slight glance over his shoulder as he called out his reply. "I have to beat that widow woman to the Rockin' R. I ought to be the one to tell my wife I just gave our ranch to another woman!"

Chapter 9

Badland
Choctaw Country, Indian Territory

Katie rubbed her neck, but even that motion did nothing to soothe the raw and burning ache of her throat. If anything, it made it worse. Actually, just thinking of her dry throat and the last time they'd had any fresh water to drink was just shy of torturous. "Didn't know Texas was quite so hot," she rasped. "Never got this hot in Indiana."

Peter flipped the reins to urge their thirsty Sookie onward. They had come a long piece since Vinita and had been so wrapped up in the affairs of Clayton Allison that they had neglected to pack extra water. "We're not in Texas yet, Katie."

She watched a fat pearl of sweat slid down the side of Peter's face. "I figured us to be almost there by now." Adjusting her seat brought no comfort as the blackness of the buggy made the inside little more than a rolling oven. "Where are we then?"

"Remember when I said we were leaving Vinita, just inside Indian Territory?"

Katie thought back and attempted a swallow. "Yes. Doesn't Texas come after Indian Territory?"

Peter's lips tipped into a half-smile. "Most folks still call this land we're in now Indian Territory. Others think it's part of Oklahoma. Whatever it is, we still haven't made it through yet."

An icy shudder slid down Katie's backbone. Leaning, she peered out of the buggy and into the scrub brushy hills that surrounded them. "You mean, there really are Indians here? Wild ones, like Mr. Allison, spoke of?"

"Maybe."

A smile danced across Katie's lips at the recollection of Clayton Allison. "Have you noticed that the closer we get to Texas, the less out of place we both seem?"

Peter coughed a dry cough. "Full of colorful characters, Texas is. Figure we'll fit right in."

Katie sucked in a lungful of air so hot that it burned her raw throat. "So where do you suppose the Indians are?"

"Well, since this is their land we're traveling across, my guess would be anywhere around here."

Thank you, God, for having the divine foresight to send Peter to help me, Your stubborn but faithful servant, on this journey. She twined her fingers together tightly to keep them from shaking.

"Why did they all move here? Because of the fine weather?" Katie's attempt at a joke fell on deaf ears as Peter stared straight ahead into the hot, unchanging hills.

"The United States government moved them all here, Katie, and most are none too happy about it." He flipped the reins again and scanned the horizon. "To most of these Indian folks, white people are the enemy. Not only to them, but to everything they love and hold dear, as well."

Katie dabbed at the sweat that tickled her forehead. "Oh." Her heart sank a bit. Even though they weren't English, both she and Peter would probably still be considered white from an Indian's perspective.

"Katie, look!"

Craning her neck, she struggled to see what Peter pointed to in the distance. Squinting, her eyes only saw the same scrubby hills. "What is it?"

"Looks to be a town," Peter said, shielding his eyes with one hand. "Where there's a town, there's water."

He licked his lips with his tongue, which was no doubt just as dry, swollen, and gritty as hers. "As long as it isn't a ghost town," he whispered.

"Thank you, God," Katie rasped, choosing to ignore the ghost town remark, as they passed a roughshod shingle nailed to a tree. "Thank you for the town of..." Katie squinted to read the shingle as they passed. "Badland." She glanced at Peter. "Badland? Did I read that right?"

"Badland it is."

Katie licked her lips again. The mere thought of water had sent a ravenous surge through her mouth and throat. Unfortunately, *that* resulted in nothing more than a dry ache that encompassed her entire neck and chest. Thinking that there might not be any more people here was too horrific a thought to bear, so she didn't think it. "The well. Let's find the well of Badland, Peter."

Sure enough, there in the center of the dusty and over-grown street sat a dilapidated well house. Katie perched on the side of the buggy, ready to dive out the moment it rolled to a stop. Peter had only just reined in Sookie before Katie dove out, hitting the ground running in her once-shiny black shoes. Hand over hand, she began hauling up the bucket.

"I find it strange," Peter started, "that we haven't seen another soul since pulling into Badland."

A dry breeze swirled down the street, bringing with it a round and rolling tumbleweed, but no hint of any nearby moisture. A derelict wooden door hung, squeaking, on a rusty hinge punctuating the eerie silence. The haunting sounds of the deserted street echoed ominously as Katie hauled the splintery bucket up over the side of the broken down well. Before she could get it to her mouth, Sookie stuck her dry black nose smack dab in the lifesaving liquid. Katie smiled. "I suppose you ought to get to go first, Sookie."

Peter's voice was more adamant than before, edging on worried. "Katie, don't you agree? Don't you find it odd? Katie?"

Tilting up the sloshing bucket, Katie ignored Peter as the remaining liquid ran down her throat in welcome gulps, soothing what was dry and healing what was cracked and aching. Katie ignored the slick horse spit that accompanied it.

"Hey, stop!" A woman's voice, peppered by a deep and rattling cough, echoed through the empty town. "Mister, stop that gal!"

Katie watched from the corner of her eye as Peter approached the woman, whose head poked out of a nearby ramshackle door. He held his hands out in peace. "I'm sorry for our intrusion ma'am, but we're mighty thirsty—"

She thrust a bent and gnarled finger out the door. "Stop her, Mister! Can't you read?"

Turning to search where she pointed, Peter caught sight of something that made him pale. "Katie, stop!" Turning on his heel as she wiped her damp lips on her sleeve, Peter dashed full force to her side. "Put the bucket down, this whole town is quarantined!"

Katie's arms went limp and the bucket fell from her hands into the dirt. A rolling, nauseous feeling surged in her stomach. Sookie, however, had no qualms about slurping up what water was left in the misbegotten bucket. "What did you say, Peter?"

Peter pointed to a pitiful excuse for a sign, also nailed to a tree. Running both hands through his hair, he brought them down hard against his sides and muttered things under his breath that she couldn't rightly understand. One thing was certain—she had never seen such a wild-eyed look on the face of her sweet Peter.

"I should have checked closer when I got that bad feeling." Stomping his foot, Peter swore an oath for the first time since she had known him.

"Peter," she admonished.

Sobering, Peter exhaled a long breath. "Can you read that sign, Katie."

Katie squinted and tried to sound out the misspelled word. "Gr—gripe." She looked to Peter for confirmation, her hopeful brows arched skyward. "Gripe. Isn't that what English people do when they are upset?" She forced an uneasy smile in an attempt to lighten the heaviness of the moment. At the same time, she willed the emotion building inside of her not to explode.

Peter's face had grown deathly pale. "That's not *gripe*, Katie. It's *grippe*. As in *the* grippe."

Katie tried to remember where she'd heard the word before, but fear fuzzed her memory. Glancing at her fingers, she realized she was trembling. Hard.

Picking up his hat, Peter shoved it back down on his head without bothering to dust it off. "That's what most people call the influenza. Shuts down whole towns and has been known to wipe out a few."

Katie gulped, but the knot that had formed in her throat refused to budge. "So it could make me sick if I catch it?"

Peter looked at her, his strong shoulders slumped. "Sick? Yes, I'd say so. At the least."

"The least?" She accepted Peter's hand and clambered back into the buggy. "What do you mean, *the least*?"

Peter snapped the reins, but didn't look at her. Sookie appeared as though leaving the well was the last thing she wanted to do, but she turned away from it grudgingly. They passed the last of the tar-paper houses before he answered her question. "It's deadly Katie. Mighty deadly." He snapped the reins again, driving them on out into the suffocating heat. "And it's catching."

"I'm glad you let Sookie drink her fill of the water," Katie said. The tremble in her voice was almost too much to handle. Her lower lip trembled and she looked down into her hands. "I'm sorry I didn't exercise more caution though, Peter."

Since leaving Badland, his thoughts had seemed miles away from where they rode together in the little Amish buggy that had already come so far. Still, he didn't turn to look at her.

Following Peter's lead, Katie stared out her own window. "Seems all you've been doing this trip is trying to save me." She didn't bother to look at him again. She couldn't. Because of her, they were now both in danger. Grave danger. Again. However, outlaws and guns weren't the enemy now. Thanks to her watery greed and gluttony, they both rolled along at the mercy of an unseen force called the grippe.

Peter forced a swallow. "Let's not talk about water."

"Okay," Katie whispered. Time passed and minutes felt like hours as the sun baked the little buggy.

Be quiet, Katie Knepp. Anything you say or do now will just make it worse. Staring out the buggy window into the scrubby hills, something in the late afternoon sun caught her attention.

She squinted and rubbed her eyes. Sure enough, something metallic glinted off the ground. Thanks to the sudden ache that cramped her throat, Katie could only point to the shiny metal.

"Railroad tracks," Peter said, perking up a bit. "How about that."

Katie wanted to smile, but it just wouldn't come.

"Katie, you're awful quiet, are you alright?"

Forcing a wan smile, she nodded. *Every fiber of my being wants to rip this covering off and fling it into the dirt*, she thought harshly. Glancing at her hands, she noticed they'd paled and begun to tremble again. *God, I'm sorry. I'm so sorry,* she prayed quickly. *I don't know what's come over me.* A chilled sweat cropped up in the small of her back. Katie shivered a sudden, violent shiver.

Peter eyed her warily. "Katie..." His voice trailed off as a makeshift station came into view. "Well, would you look at that little depot. Looks like they're unloading a couple of passengers, how interesting."

Katie rubbed at her eyes. "Why here?" Her voice wouldn't rise above a whisper.

"I reckon they have destinations that aren't close to either of the big depots along the line," Peter mused. "Oh, nope. Just one passenger is getting off. The other was a worker helping her with her bag." Peter sat upright, studying the display as Sookie slowed to a walk. "And it's just a few little train cars long. How about that."

Slouched back against the seat and closing her eyes, Katie rubbed her aching wrists.

"Oh Katie, look there. That'll raise your spirits." Peter reined Sookie to a stop.

When she opened her eyes, Katie discovered that everything in her vision had blurred, the edges furring and blending until just a mishmash of color remained. "We're stopping?"

"Annie," Peter called, jumping out of the buggy. "Is that really you?"

Feeling poorly, Katie listed on the buggy seat. "Annie? My sister? Are you here?" Fumbling with her feet and her dress, Katie somehow made her way out of the confounded buggy. She tried to call out, holding onto the buggy for support. "Annie? Are you really here?" The words registered as unintelligible, even to her ears.

The familiar voice that mirrored her own came from everywhere. "Katie! Katie? Oh Peter, catch her!"

It's not a dream. My Annie is here. The blackness swept in from everywhere blocking out her vision. *Like an angry ocean wave on the docks of New York City,* she thought as her knees turned to applesauce. *Or like Clayton Allison's hair waving back from his forehead.* Then, everything was gone.

Chapter 10

Oklahoma Territory

A cool hand rested on Katie's forehead. "Oh Peter, she's burning up."

Katie felt herself being lifted from the ground, but exhaustion sapped her ability to talk. Instead, she mumbled.

"She's trying to talk. Let me lean closer to hear what my sister is saying."

Peter's booming voice was gruff. "Stop, Annie. It's the grippe and it's catching." He laid her on the buggy seat. "Stay as far away as you can."

Sookie jerked the buggy to the tune of the snapping reins, sending a wave of nausea crashing over Katie. A groan escaped her parched lips.

"She's my sister," Annie argued. "I'll take care of her, God willing I won't get it." The rim of the tin cup touched her lips. "Here Katie. Drink."

"Are all you Knepp women stubborn from birth or is it a learned behavior?"

No, let Peter drink. He's so thirsty. She could feel herself mumbling, and she could hear the garbled words. *Please, let Peter drink.*

Peter's voice sounded far away, as though he was talking in a dream. "She's trying to let me have the water first, Annie. Tell her I already drank my fill of the water that you were so wise to bring."

The cool drops on her lips and tongue brought little relief as every part of her body began to ache in a way it never had before.

"Stop the buggy, Peter. We have to stop."

"Don't you think we should get on to the next town? So she'll have a bed, and a doctor—"

Annie interrupted him. "Stop the buggy, Peter. She's getting worse by the moment. My sister needs rest and she can't get it in this jostling buggy."

Katie felt herself being lifted out of the buggy. *I love you, Peter.*

"She's not making any sense." Even to her fever-thick ears, Katie recognized the desperation in Peter's voice. "God, please don't take her away from me. Forgive me, Father, for bringing her on this trip."

A freezing chill gripped Katie as someone stripped her of her dress, leaving her writhing in her skivvies on the hard-packed earth. She felt the pebbles and the pokey grass against her exposed skin, but strangely wasn't worried about modesty. The issue of the clutching cold fingers that seemed to have wrapped themselves about her very bones was much more pressing.

"This is why we shouldn't be on this trip, Katie," Peter whispered as he covered her over with one of the quilts from the buggy. Katie's arms contracted to her chest and her body shook with chills. *I'm slipping away, I can feel it. Help me, please. God, don't forget me. Remember me, please. Stubborn Katie Knepp.*

Annie's voice sounded farther away than ever before. A rush of cold swept over her body as the quilt was jerked off. "Her fever's too high. We have to cool her down or she's going to die. Bring me the water, Peter. Then, please build a fire for you and me."

Peter's voice was a quiet whisper, growing quieter with

each passing word. "Watch your, sister Annie. Here comes an Indian." As he finished speaking, only silence remained.

The brightness of the moon was the first thing Katie saw when she finally opened her eyes. Crickets chirped and lightning bugs flitted about the campsite as she struggled to focus. A symphony of night sounds seemed amplified to her ears. "Am I dead?" she asked to no one.

Annie's face appeared over her, tears shining on her full cheeks. "You certainly gave us cause to wonder." Her lips parted into a grateful smile as she tucked the quilt around her ill sister. The night breeze was cool, but not freezing. Katie shivered and pulled the quilt up to her chin. "Peter?"

"He's here. Been up by your side since you took sick. Praying and tending to you." She glanced over to another quilt-covered body nearby. "I think it best if we let him sleep. Do you need me to wake him?"

Katie shook her head. "I'm glad you're here."

"So am I," Annie agreed, stirring a pot over the fire. "But I am even more that glad she is here."

"She?"

Annie nodded toward the flickering firelight as Katie struggled to prop herself up on her elbows. "Her name is Mah-Chetta-Wookey," she whispered.

Her tanned face, illuminated by the soft glow, bore no trace of a smile as she ground something in a bowl. Her grinding complete, she stuck out one arm and dumped the contents into the pot that Annie stirred over their fire.

"Mah-Chetta-Wookey." Katie twisted her tongue around the foreign words. The Indian woman seemed to stare right through her as Katie stared back, impolitely, just as her mother had taught her not to do. The Indian woman's hair fell around her shoulders in thick plaits which were each wrapped in red cloth. A swirling breeze made a hidden feather flutter out from behind one long, inky braid. Not fully understanding anything, Annie turned her attention back to her sister.

"She saved your life, Katie. With a remedy, she learned from her people."

Everything was fuzzy. "Her people?"

"The Comanche."

Feeling dizzy again, Katie laid back and nestled down into the quilt.

Annie's voice was urgent. "Katie?"

Mah-Chetta-Wookey's unsmiling face was there, floating in and out of her vision. "Thank you, Mah... Mah..." The ghost of a smile haunted Mah-Chetta-Wookey's lips as Katie gave over to the incorrigible exhaustion once again.

Katie drank the broth from the pot, steeped from the root that Mah-Chetta-Wookey had pounded for her. As she gulped down the bland liquid, her covering fell away. Her hair was left blowing free in the wild breezes of Indian Territory. With another drink, they formed into red-wrapped braids, just like Mah-Chetta wore.

"What's happening," Katie cried, stretching her arms out before her. Nobody was there to answer. As she watched, her skin took on the hue of every color of the wild sunset. An unseen drum thumped out a rhythm that pulsed through her, matching the beating of her heart. Katie saw herself from afar, much like she was floating far above her body.

She watched herself as she stood alone in the wilderness, the land sprawling out before her. The sense of adventure beckoned with the waving of the trees. The sun in the sky warmed her back as the rain fell from clouds beneath her. "I will live," she declared. Looking down, Katie saw that she was a part of everything and everything was a part of her. An eagle shrieked overhead.

With a gasp, Katie awoke in a cold sweat. Checking her arms, she sighed. They were the right color. "Wait, why can I see my arms?" Peeking under the quilt, Katie flushed. Somewhere in the back of her mind danced the fuzzy memory of someone stripping her dress from her body. *How long have I been in my underwear*, she wondered, glancing around the campsite. Feeling as though eyes were upon her, she searched for her traveling companions.

Peter was asleep, snoring softly under a quilt, nearest the buggy. Annie was stretched out, facing the campfire, the light flickering on her weary face. Rubbing her eyes, Katie peered into the darkness around the edge of camp. Sure enough, a pair of gentle eyes shone softly.

"I knew you would live."

Suddenly self-conscious, Katie pulled the quilt tighter up to her chin even though she felt the woman already knew her on a level that few, if any, ever would. "I owe you my life. Thank you."

She smiled and rose from the shadows. Slowly, Mah-Chetta walked with an easy, rolling gait to where Katie rested. "I leave you the medicine. Keep drinking broth. Give to anyone else sick."

Katie couldn't help herself. "Why, you're pregnant. And still, you treated me."

The smile faded from the Indian woman's face. "I follow my husband's war trail to where he surrendered at Fort Sill. I too will go willingly into bonds."

"Is your husband Quanah Parker?"

No emotion registered on Mah's finely featured face. She nodded.

"I know the man who escorted your husband. He was mighty sick with himself. May well have ruined his life, as far as I could tell." *Why are you making excuses for Clayton Allison, Katie?*

Mah rose and stood, illuminated by firelight. "Our lives as we knew them are now over. I have nothing but a future of slavery at the hands of the white man before me, and before my child." Gently, she placed her hands on her bulging stomach. "But I helped you on my way to my life of prison."

Katie tried to wrap her newly fever-free mind around Mah's cryptic words. She wasn't successful. "Why don't you go somewhere else?"

Mah's face never changed expression. "There is nowhere free left to go for The People." She stood silently for a moment. "Now, *you* will live free for me. And for my child."

Katie nodded. "I will." Not knowing the protocol, or if one even existed, to seal her promise to the Indian woman, Katie weakly offered up her hand to shake.

Mah looked down at her for a moment, the firelight flickering off her face in a way that Katie knew would burn this moment into her memory forever. "Live free for me, Katie," Mah whispered. Then, she was gone.

"I didn't come all this way to be your nursemaid you know."

Katie awoke to Annie's chipper joshing. The familiar warmth that came with being near her twin spread through her weak but strangely rejuvenated body.

"Were you scared?" Katie shook her head. Her words still weren't making as much sense as she intended for them to.

"Of course I was!" Annie laughed as she tended to the little camp chores that needed doing. "But I have a little sister who braved the streets of New York City for Rumspringa before heading south to such a wild place as Texas. I couldn't let you show me up now, could I?"

Katie paused a long while, letting the words form themselves in her mind, before trusting them on her tongue. "No, you certainly couldn't. You had to come see if you could get the grippe, too." A bird called low and long from a branch just overhead. "I'm so glad you're here, Annie." *And I'm so glad I'm going live. I'm not sure if I would have if you hadn't showed up when you did. Peter would have kept going, right past Ma-Chetta and her miracle root.* Thoughts swished fiercely in her mind, but wouldn't come to fruition so she could speak them. Staring at Annie, who seemed to already know, Katie let the tears of thankfulness run down her cheeks in relieved rivulets.

Annie's eyes gleamed in the soft rays of morning sunlight. She patted Katie's hand. "I brought news."

With a sniffle, Katie pushed herself up as quickly as she could manage. Annie's words brought her suddenly awake although her arms were still a bit shaky. "Oh?"

Sucking in her bottom lip, Annie slipped over to the campfire and removed the coffee pot, which was which was boiling over the rim. Turning back to face her, Annie looked as though she might burst. "Ma and Pa are coming. To join us. In Texas!"

Katie stammered over her words, praying they would untangle themselves in her brain and just come out the way she intended for them to. "What? How? Why?" *I thought I caught something in Ma's eye when I shared my heart with her back in Gasthof.*

"They just left Indiana. Pa said when you caused such an uproar, they decided to put the Bible and family before Ordnung." Annie skipped back over to Katie and swept both her sister's hands into hers. "We will be a New Order of family in Old Amarillo. A whole new sense of freedom!"

Forcing a swallow, Katie tried to process the news her sister had risked her own life to bring. "Quanah Parker's wife was traveling her husband's war trail, pregnant and alone. She was bound for a life of imprisonment, for her *and* her child." Katie sobered despite the overwhelmingly glorious news Annie had brought. "And still she went on."

"She is an amazing person." Annie's thin lips twitched into a smile. "She doctored Sookie's burned ankles with a salve, too."

Katie nodded before she continued, speaking words that were hushed and brimming with reverence. "When Mah-Chetta could have just left, run away and started her young life over somewhere else, she followed her husband willingly to prison." Katie looked up at Annie and tightened her fingers around those of her sister. Her tears threatened to spill over from the fringe of lashes that held them at bay. "Free takes on a new meaning now, doesn't it?"

Chapter 11

North Texas

"He was right," Peter mused, scanning the landscape. He had exited the buggy at the first sign of the fencing. "It looks like ranchers *are* trying to keep Clayton Allison out of Texas." Gleaming strands of barbed wire, punctuated every so often with a misbegotten branch or post, stretched from horizon to horizon, choking the north Texas plains with its silvery, glistening barbs. Finally, Peter turned back to face Katie and Annie. Slowly, he removed his hat and scratched his head. "Do you suppose I missed a turn somewhere?"

Annie shook her head. "No, we are on the trail. It just goes through this barbed wire fence and onto this person's land."

Ignoring the oppressive heat from the ever-present sun as best she could, Katie glanced at her sister. "How do you know how to follow a trail? I have been having trouble keeping up with it all along the way."

Smug, Annie was eager to answer. "I followed the trail all the way here and I have been watching Peter's driving."

Before Katie could turn the conversation into an argument, Peter broke in. "How *did* you do it all alone, Annie?" Even though he engaged Annie in conversation, Katie could see the look in Peter's eyes. In his mind, he was going back over the trail for as far back as he could remember, wondering if he missed a branch that would lead them around this endless swath of barbed wire. She smiled. *I'm coming to know him, and understand him, quite well.*

Annie, her face glowing beneath the veil of sweat, shrugged. "Well, I mended dresses for an English woman in Illinois." Annie paused and tapped her finger to her chin. "No, she wasn't so much English as she was something else…" Her face suddenly brightened. "She was a Gypsy. Her name was Minerva, in Elizabethtown."

Katie opened her mouth to speak, but only a strange little squeak escaped her tightened throat.

Annie continued. "Well, once I had enough money for train fare," she relayed, "I came along by train. I suppose I *rode the rails*, as the English call it." Annie giggled, obviously delighting in her own adventure story. Having always been the more subdued of the Knepp sisters, Annie having trumped her sister in an adventure story made a scarlet hue grow within Katie's cheeks.

Katie ducked her head and sighed. "Sometimes I wish I was more like you, Annie."

"Adventurous?" Annie's eyes gleamed as she taunted her baby sister.

Katie shook her head. "No. Logical." The girls dissolved into a fit of giggles.

Peter hung his head, his black hat casting a shadow over his smiling, angular face. Finally, he lifted his eyes to Katie and Annie. "Well, I can't recall there being any other branch off this here trail. And," he studied carefully the fencing that disappeared into both horizons. "There's going to be no going around. We are going to have to go through."

Katie pushed her way out of the buggy. A rogue breeze whistled across the high plains, swirling the thick, golden dust around her feet. Careful of the barbs, Katie grasped the topmost of the three taut metal strands. "How will we go through this, Peter?" She glanced at him.

Peter stepped to her side. "Very carefully." He pointed to the rickety posts that held the strands of wire. "The fencing is nailed in here. We will pull out the nails, drive over the flat fencing, and then nail it back into place."

Katie took a step back, shielding her face with one hand from both the sun and the dust. "Can I do anything to help you?" The sudden swirl of dust kicked up into what looked like a miniature cyclone. Grains of sand pelted her face and Annie covered Sookie's eyes.

When it passed, the trio watched the tiny twister snake its way along the flat Texas plains until it just sort of winked out. Peter shook his head and stepped to the nearest post. He pulled the 3 ½-inch brim of his round black hat down low. "No, no help necessary now," he answered, straining to pull out the first nail from the tough wood. As it released, he glanced up and flashed a quick and smiling wink at Katie. "But thank you for the kind offer, though."

A burst of fluttering butterflies took flight in Katie's stomach as she watched Peter work. The muscles in his arms flexed and strained beneath his deep blue shirt as he took care not to break the post or bend the nails. Beads of sweat slid down from his hairline, catching the angle of his jaw, before falling away. Katie chewed her lip. *He has worked so hard this entire trip—for me.*

The strands of barbed wire went slack as Peter removed the last nail. "Well, I'm going to need to take the nails out of one more post, maybe two." Swiping his sleeve across his forehead, Peter held the nails out to Katie. "Would you like to hold these?"

Nodding, Katie accepted the handful of metal spikes. She wasn't quite sure why she couldn't meet Peter's gaze. However she knew the heat that pulsed warmly through her body wasn't just because of the harsh Texas sun.

"So will I get to see you two be married soon?" Annie's soft voice mingled with the breeze. "He looks at you the same way Pa looks at Ma, Katie."

Ducking her head, Katie fingered the handful of nails. One poked into her palm. "He's told me that he loves me, but won't let me tell of my feelings for him until we reach Amarillo."

Annie giggled. "That sounds about right."

Katie was taken aback. "What do you mean?"

"Oh Katie, you know you have always hated to wait for anything. You see what you want, you get it. You get an idea in your head, you make it happen. Right then, without waiting." Annie giggled.

I suppose I have.

"Now Peter is forcing you to wait and that makes you want it all the more, doesn't it?"

Katie's eyes widened. "How did you know?"

Annie reached and patted her sister on the shoulder. "We're twins, remember?"

With a grunt, Peter held the last nail heroically above his head. The barbed, metal strands fell to the ground. "Got it!"

Exchanging a grin, Katie and Annie raced back to the buggy.

"Now drive carefully," Peter warned. "I'll guide Sookie so her hooves don't crunch any of the barbs."

"Alright."

Lifting the reins, Katie clicked her tongue quietly. "Come on, Sookie. Be careful, Sookie." Annie sat beside her, back erect, as Peter guided them over the fence.

"What purpose do you figure these fences serve?" Annie wondered aloud. "Perhaps to keep the Texans in?" she joshed.

Katie felt the corners of her mouth twitch upward, despite her concentration, as she steered Sookie's reins. "Or maybe it is to keep the Amish out?"

Annie gasped. "We made it!"

Not bothering to help the Knepp girls out of the buggy, Peter immediately went to work mending the fence he'd just taken down. "Katie, could you bring the nails I gave you please?" Quicker than it took to take them down, Peter had the strands nailed back into place. He stepped back to admire his handiwork. "There now. I think I even got them nailed up a might tighter than they were at first." Turning to Katie, he brushed his thumb across her cheek. "The English may even hire me to mend fences in Amarillo." His face cracked into a handsome, crooked smile.

Katie blinked. *Tell him now, Katie Knepp. We're here in Texas, maybe this is close enough.* "Peter, I—" she began. From behind him, a long shadow grew from over a little hill. Katie took a step back, her appetite for conversation squelched.

Slowly, the shadow grew longer and longer still until it cloaked Peter.

"Um, Peter? Someone's there."

Whirling on his heel, Peter turned to face the man who still shrouded him in his massive shadow. Katie watched as the stranger on the little hill lifted his hand to his mouth and plucked a cigarette from his lips. The breeze fluttered his coat as he stood unmoving, staring at them. The pair of pistols that hung on his hips caught the sun and shone out, making Katie squint against the blinding metallic glare. *Silver devils*, Katie thought. *Someone once described pistols like that as silver devils.* She let her gaze travel up the man and focus on his cold, staring eyes. *And now I understand why.*

Flicking the cigarette through the dry air, the stranger spoke. His voice was dark and raspy. "Oneida."

Katie stared at the stranger and pondered his cryptic word. The silence that hung thick in the air unnerved her considerably. She glanced at Peter, who also stared at the stranger in silence. Finally, she blew out a huff. "What did you say, mister?"

His face didn't change expression as his eyes locked on hers as his hands arched over his pistols. "You said you were going to Amarillo," he snarled. "The original name is Oneida—Amarillo will never stick."

Before Katie could respond, the stranger continued.

> *"Oneida.*
> *Once I saw your morning star, a-sitting in the sky.*
> *All the wildness of this land made calm as you passed by."*

Arching her eyebrows skyward, Katie glanced at Peter. Again, she opened her mouth to speak only to be interrupted by the poetry-wielding gunfighter, his voice louder this time.

> *"I ponder life, and death and such*
> *and know that that I'll suffer it as much.*
> *And when that lonely night doth falls,*
> *and that lonely night bird calls,*
> *I'll be home again—in Oneida."*

Katie cocked her head and skimmed her mental scriptures. *That sounds like it should be Biblical.* "That's beautiful, Mister."

The stranger's grizzled face cracked into a broken grin. "Thank you, penned it myself."

Katie released her hands, which she'd unknowingly was wringing at her middle. "So you're a poet. Phew!" She blew up a lock of mahogany bangs that had fallen from beneath her covering. "Thank God. And we thought you were going to shoot us."

Peter and Annie's voices rang out through the sudden stillness in unison. "Katie!"

Slipping into their native tongue, Katie whispered back a response in choppy, barking syllables. "Well, we did."

The stranger dropped his hands, allowing his duster to flip back over the silver devils. He stepped down the little hill toward them. "Never killed a man that didn't need killin'." Extending his gnarled hand to Peter, he continued, "Like William said: *Love all, trust a few, do wrong to no one.*" His lips pulled back as he spoke, revealing his straight, perfectly white teeth below his equally white mustache. The tiny stem of a weed, the head of which looked a bit like a feathery windmill, was gritted there, poking out just beneath one white curl. "Cabe Adams. Pleased to make your acquaintance."

"I'm Peter Wagler. This here is Katie and Annie Knepp." Peter's voice, which had taken on a hint of the Texan's twang, interrupted her studying of the man. "Sorry to be crossin' your ranch Mr. Adams, but the trail ended straight into your place."

Cabe released Peter's hand and nodded, staring off into the distance. "Yeah, working on getting that fixed. Made the trip to Fort Elliott two weeks ago. Filed my land plat at Texas General Land Office. Once those fools see that the road ends smack-dab into my spread, they'll have to make a move to reroute the road."

Peter nodded as though he understood what the Cabe was talking about. Katie, however, just stared at the gunman.

Cabe ran a finger over his mustache, unconsciously curling the end with one finger as he spoke.

"So they tell me they can't help me, but send me over to file my paper at the land office in Oneida. Which I did." Finally, he glanced at Peter with clear and piercing eyes. "That's Amarillo. Now, I just have to wait."

"I'm relieved to hear that we're so close," Peter mused.

Cabe cocked his head. "Well, it ain't exactly spittin' distance—"

Katie shook her head, still trying to catch up in the conversation. "Who's William, Mr. Adams?"

Cabe turned his attention back to Katie. "Do what?"

"William. Who said that about love, trust, and doing wrong." Her cheeks heated. "Er, well, maybe it was about *not* doing wrong."

Icy blue eyes twinkling, Cabe shifted his weight so he was facing Katie completely. "Why that's William Shakespeare, darlin'. He is one of the finest poets ever to walk the earth. Have you read his work?"

Katie shook her head. "I don't read so well."

"That's a pity. A young gal with an ear for poetry such as yourself would make a fine teacher somewhere. Or writer."

Gazing at the eclectic man with wonder, Katie let loose her curious tongue. "What are you doing way out here, Mr. Adams? You ought to be minding a class in a schoolhouse somewhere yourself, since you can read and write."

Annie sucked in a sharp breath somewhere from over her shoulder. In their shared language, she began to utter so only Katie could hear. "Ma would faint dead away if she heard such boldness on your tongue!"

Cabe interrupted Annie's admonishment of her sister.

"Well, it ain't no matter young lady. Fact is that presently, I run one of the largest cattle outfits in the Lone Star State. Largest on the Llano Estacado. But if you're wonderin' why I'm out on this corner of my ranch right now, it just so happens I'm setting up a graveyard."

Peter audibly gulped. "A—um, an, well—a graveyard, Mr. Adams?"

Cabe nodded. "Yes, sir. Buryin' the last group of folks that come through here and cut my fence." He pointed to the little hill from whence he'd come.

Not bothering to be meek, Katie gave over to her curiosity. Again. Clutching the skirt of her dress in her hands, she trudged across the short expanse to the little hill and trotted up easily. What she saw made her stomach knot and tighten. Sure enough, four empty graves were visible just down the far side of the slope. A shiny spade was stuck like a victor's flag in the mound of fresh grave dirt, and four pairs of boots stuck out from beneath a bedraggled tarp nearby.

The juices sloshing in Katie's freshly healed stomach lurched into her throat, leaving a burning trail in their wake. "Oh," she gurgled, bringing her hand up sharply to her mouth. "Oh, my." She knew she should pray, but the situation was so confounded, she wasn't sure what to pray, or for whom. A deafening silence filled the plains as Katie plodded back to face the group, her eyes downcast, unwilling and unable to meet the equally curious stares of Peter and Annie.

"I'm thinking of calling it Dead Man's Gulch Graveyard. What do you folks think?" Cabe's eyes glimmered as he slowly drew his gaze from Katie to Peter to Annie.

Minutes clicked by. After what seemed an eternity, Cabe laughed. "No worries now. Those men waiting to be planted weren't near as nice as you folks. They didn't make a move to fix my fence after they cut it, so I figured them to be cattle rustlers. Then, they didn't even know any Shakespeare." Cabe shook his head and pulled a long, rolled cigarette from his shirt pocket. "Sometimes I wonder if old Will was right. Maybe hell *is* empty and all the devils are here." Striking a flint, he lit his smoke. "Or getting here as quick as they can."

Sensing that she should be a bit offended but not sure why, Katie squared her shoulders. "We don't look like cattle rustlers!"

Cabe drew in a deep breath, transforming the end of his cigarette into a glowing orange orb. He exhaled and hid a snort. "Lil' sister, don't take no offense now, but it don't look like y'all could rustle your own buggy horse."

Hmmm.

Cabe started toward the little hill. "Well, folks. I welcome you to continue on your way across my ranch. Stop at the house if you like. Marge is fixin' supper for the boys. Tell her to save me a plate, but I won't be back till late." He ducked his head and inhaled the rest of his smoke in a crackling, glowing breath. "Time for me to get these fellers planted. Do unto others," he muttered to himself.

Katie finished as he walked by her. "As you would have them do unto you. Luke 6:13."

Cabe paused. He fingered his mustache a moment before speaking. "Our Lord, the greatest poet of all." He flashed Katie a wide grin. "To thine own self be true, Katie Knepp." Reaching into his back pocket, he produced a small leather bound book. Giving it one last loving brush with his thumb, he offered it to her.

The letters on the front had at one time been stamped

in gold. *This must be quite old*, Katie figured. *The only gold that remains now is in just a few corners of the letters here.* She studied the little book bound in leather, worn smooth over the years. "Shakespeare Sonnets," she sounded out carefully.

Cabe brought his fingers to the tip of his hat. "Welcome to Texas, y'all."

Chapter 12

Broken O Cattle Company Ranch
Llano Estacado

"That must be the house." Katie craned her neck to take in the full expanse of the wooden abode. "I didn't know ranchers had such big houses." She turned on the seat and adjusted her covering. "You don't suppose they let the cows sleep inside at night, do you?"

Peter stifled a laugh. "I believe what we're seeing is quite a few buildings, but from way back here they all look like one big house. There's probably the main ranch house where Mr. Adams lives with his wife—"

"Marge," Katie and Annie interrupted together.

Peter smiled. "Yes, of course, Marge. Then those there are probably bunk houses for the cowboys that Mr. Adams has hired on to work the cattle." Peter snapped the reins over Sookie's back and pointed to a row of buildings. The black mare's high steps were closing the distance between them and the ranch house quickly. "And don't forget the barn, stables, tack houses, loafing sheds—"

"I think I understand now." Katie patted his exposed wrist and dropped her voice low. "Welcome to Texas, Peter." She hoped he caught her underlying meaning. The sideways wink he flashed her spoke of his quiet understanding.

Annie piped up from the backseat. "The first thing I'm

going to do when we reach the house is to get a big, cold, wet drink."

Katie forced a swallow at Annie's mention of water, her dry throat scratchy. The fact that their water had run out the day before had kept any mention of drinking to a minimum. However with the sight unfolding before them, the talk of water that had been suppressed began to flow freely.

"I think I'll pour a dipperful over my head first," Peter mused. "It won't be rain, but almost as good. How about you, Katie?"

Katie glanced at the faithful buggy horse that had brought them from the gentle Indiana woods out to the middle of nowhere, all on her prayer. "First thing I'm going to do is lead Sookie up to the most inviting watering hole. Or trough. Whatever they have for horses to drink from on Texas cattle ranches."

"Here we are." Peter didn't even attempt to rein in Sookie as they passed the bewildered cattlemen but drove her, buggy and all, right up to the trough in front of the bunkhouse. The black mare wasted no time in dipping her nose right in and sucking up the sweet liquid. Only then did Peter climb out of the buggy himself.

The group of young cowboys, decked out in hats, spurs, boots, and pistols, gathered around. As Peter helped Annie climb out of the buggy, Katie noticed a few cowboys elbowing and pointing. Their curious smiles turned their lips upward on their weathered faces. She recognized their obvious inquisitiveness right off, as it had been her own that led them here in the first place.

With Annie safely out of the buggy, Peter turned his attention back to Katie. "Are you ready?" He offered her his arm.

Feeling a bit self-conscious beneath the weight of the cowboys' curious stares, Katie took it cautiously. "Where are we going?" Her voice came out little more than a whisper.

"Now with the horse watered, you're free to drink your fill." He winked at her again, relaxing all the knots that had formed in her stomach over the course of the journey. The butterflies took flight again and Katie welcomed the strange, comforting warmth that spread through her when Peter was near.

Normally quick-witted and armed with a snappy comeback, Katie was at a loss for words with his sweet gesture. "Thank you," was all she could muster through her blustery brain. *I love you, Peter. I've always loved you...*

Finally, one of the cowboys summoned up the gumption to introduce himself. Stepping forward, he jingled musically. His smile, wide on his tanned face, spoke the universal language of friendliness. "Howdy y'all. I'm Guthrie, George Guthrie. Welcome to the Broken O Cattle Company."

Peter took his proffered hand and shook it hard. "Thank you for the welcome. I'm Peter Wagler and this is Katie Knepp and her sister, Annie." Peter gestured with his free hand, but Katie had slipped off his arm, unnoticed. She snickered from behind the cowboy's wooden water barrel on the porch.

"Katie?"

Seizing the moment, Katie sprang up, the filled dipper in hand. "Here's *your* treat, Peter," she cried. In an instant, she had tipped the dipper as close to the top of Peter's head as she could manage, giving a fair soaking to her beau.

Peter's eyes registered the surprise for only a moment before a wide grin overtook his handsome face. Reaching out, he swept Katie into his arms. She didn't resist as Peter pulled her close, closer than she'd ever been before, with a glorious and triumphant shout. "We've made it, Katie girl!" Twirling her around, tiny droplets of water sprayed from the both of them, no doubt giving a sprinkling to those nearby. Katie threw her head back and laughed. "We've made it!" Peter's echoing shout brought a cheerful whoop from the cowmen.

"A long time on the trail will do that to a body," one whispered to another.

The world was spinning when Peter finally sat her down. "We've made it," he whispered again, his mouth so near to her ear that goose bumps cropped up on her neck as his warm breath caressed her face and neck.

We've really and truly made it. Thank you, God. Thank you.

Annie coughed from the porch. "I think I'll take the dusty water jugs from the buggy and go draw some fresh water from the well. This water barrel seems to be tainted or something." The ghost of a knowing smile flickered across her lips.

Breaking from his trance, Peter looked up at Annie. "I can do that, Annie."

Annie waved her hand and hurried to the buggy, which was attached to a still-drinking Sookie. "I made it most of the way here without a man's help. I expect I can find a well on a ranch by myself." She had a light skip in her step as she trotted around the corner of the bunk house.

Suddenly very aware that she was clasped in Peter's arms in front of an army of cowmen, Katie flushed. "I'd best go help my sister," she muttered. Shaking her head to clear the Peter-induced fog from her mind, she rounded the corner. *Maybe the moment will return when Peter and I find ourselves alone together at some point*, she figured. Searching the area for the well house, Katie got an eyeful. Skidding to a halt and almost tripping over her own feet, she watched her unobtrusive sister Annie capture the full attention of the handsome cowboy George Guthrie.

George, taller than Annie by six inches or so, reminded Katie of her first crush back at Gasthof Village—Joseph Graber. She licked her lips and took in the tall drink of water as he brought a blush to Annie's cheeks. Lanky, he looked like a rope, knotted in all the right places, giving him the air of what a cowboy should be, but she had only ever heard about. Reaching into the well, George drew up the splintery bucket and filled Annie's empty water jugs, his shy smile matching hers. Handsomely dimpled, George's angular jaw gave him a likable quality immediately, like someone you could turn to if you were in trouble—or if you simply needed a friend.

George said something, his dark eyebrows arched thoughtfully. Annie answered with a nod, and George tipped his chin upward and turned. Seeing her chance, Katie dashed to her sister's side as the cowboy, his chest puffed and a swagger in his hips, marched toward the corral.

"Annie!"

Annie's eyes glistened with a never-before-seen spark when she finally managed to pull her attention away from the retreating cowboy. "He's boss wrangler, whatever that means," she whispered, clearly wanting to watch George instead of talk to her. Annie's gaze fluttered back toward the corral. "He's like no man I've ever met, Katie."

Peter's face filled Katie's mind the same way a reminiscent dream fills the homesick thoughts of a traveler. "I understand, sister."

"He said I have an adventuresome spirit. And asked if I'd

like to watch what he does for work." Her voice was wistful. "Then if I was up for it, he would take me on a tour of the ranch."

Are those tears in Annie's eyes? "Well, what did you say?"

"I said okay!" Annie squeaked, reaching for Katie's hand. "Come on. Let's go see what he does."

As if on cue, a handful of equally lanky cowboys meandered over to the busiest end of the corral. Katie and Annie peeked through the fence. "What are they doing?" Katie asked.

"I don't know, but that horse they have in that little, tiny piece of the corral looks angry. And wild." Annie's eyes glistened as George and his fellow cowboys did things all around the skittish horse. Climbing up to the top rung Seeing them staring, one cowman broke from the bunch and sauntered over to where they stood.

"Howdy ladies, I'm Jim. Jim Guthrie, George's brother."

Katie studied him. "Younger or older?"

Jim rested his booted foot on the lowest rung of the pole fence and leaned against it. A bemused twinkle in his coffee-brown eyes, he studied Katie right back. "Well younger, but that don't mean nothin'. I'm the smarter Guthrie of the pair of us."

"Oh?" Annie asked a dash of haughtiness in her voice. "Is that so?"

Katie hid a smile. *She is quite taken with George.*

Jim nodded, the brim of his straw hat brushing the fence. "Yup. You certainly don't see me gettin' up on that wild mustang, ma'am."

"Ride a wild—mustang?" Annie glanced from Jim to where George was perched on the fence above the snorting and stamping horse. "Katie, he's going to ride it!"

The world ground to a halt as George lowered himself onto the back of the angry horse. When the mustang felt George's weight on her back she went wild, bucking and pawing at her enclosure, whinnying in a way Katie had never before heard from the tame, gentled Indiana horses. Her eyes widened thoughtfully. *I'm liking Texas more and more.*

Grinning, George flashed a wink at Annie from beneath his angled, sweat-stained black hat. "Let 'er go, boys!"

The gate to the chute exploded open as man and horse, in an epic showdown, each struggled to best the other. The mustang, small in stature but big in willpower, sought to throw George high and hard.

"If he's thrown, the mustang will stomp him to bits," Annie breathed, a look of awe on her wide-eyed face.

George proved a worthy opponent to the bucking and leaping mustang.

"Why is he doing this," Annie asked, mostly to herself.

Katie steeled her jaw. "He wants to feel it, to share it for just a few fleeting seconds."

"Share and feel what?"

Katie looked at her sister. It was high time she opened the door that Annie was still hiding behind. "A moment of true wildness. The wild whirlwind offered by the mustang. The same thing I prayed for and followed my heart south for. To feel wild. And alive."

The sense of a fog cleared from Annie's eyes. At once, Katie knew her sister now truly understood, thanks to handsome George and one wild mustang.

Both girls focused their attention on the scene unfurling in the corral. "I'm sure the seconds feel like hours," Annie mused.

"You're sure what feels like hours?"

"Every second George is on that horse."

Katie nodded. "I never knew a horse, mustang or not, that could move in such a manner," she whispered. Sure enough, the little ball of fire jumped with all four feet off the ground so high, that Katie was positive she could run underneath both George and horse without being touched.

Amazingly, George's hat had successfully stayed on his head even as his body whipped back and forth, round and round with the motion of the mustang. One hand held high above his head, George's grin flashed every time the mustang spun round their way.

Jim let out a whoop as the mustang, now covered in foam, quit bucking and trotted around the fence in a nervous circle. "That's why we call you Crackerjack, brother," he shouted over the din of the cheering cowboys.

George slid off the green broke filly and swaggered over to where they stood, tucking in the front of his shirt. *I see why he's so proud*, Katie thought. *Anyone who can do that...*

Though completely out of character, Annie spoke first. "That was very impressive." She grinned at the rosy-cheeked cowboy. "Crackerjack."

"That horse came in this morning with the other horses we rounded up to get ready for the drive," George "Crackerjack" Guthrie explained. "Bucked off everyone else who tried to ride her so far." He ducked his head, but his grin still shone. "Guess you brought me luck, Miss Annie."

Katie noticed her sister's fingers start to tremble. "Now what happens to her?"

Crackerjack's grin melted into a friendly, crooked smile. "Well, now she's mine. I'll ride her on the drive to Santa Fe."

Katie glanced around the dusty ranch. It seemed everything

was dusty since arriving in Texas. She watched as some cowboys shod horses outside the barn, while others banged at scraps of metal for reasons unknown. *This life could certainly become addicting...* A flash of Logan Dawson's handsome face and swirl of hair swept through her mind. *I wonder if Logan will be roping and gentling wild mustangs up at the Powder River Ranch in Montana?*

Feeling a bit guilty for letting her mind wander to another man, Katie pushed the rogue thought of Logan and his swirl back far away to the deepest recesses of her mind, where it belonged.

There. Now what was I looking at... At once, Katie's gaze fell upon another larger pen. Inside, one cowboy tossed a looped rope into a throng of clumped up, jittery horses while other cowmen sat on the fence and cheered him on.

"And those men there," Katie tilted her chin. "Are they trying to settle their mounts for the journey to Santa Fe, as you did?" She glanced back at Crackerjack, who still looked longingly at her sister and appeared not to have even heard her.

Jim nudged him. "What? Oh, yes. Yes ma'am," Crackerjack stammered. "Say, would you ladies like a tour of the Broken O?"

Katie opened her mouth to accept, but Annie beat her to an answer. "I'd love to."

Sucking in her bottom lip to hide her smile, Katie nodded. "So would I. Thank you."

"Why is the Broken O driving cattle to Santa Fe when you're right here next to a railroad that goes, well, to Santa Fe?"

Annie never took her eyes off Crackerjack as they roamed the cattle ranch.

Tipping his hat up with one finger, Crackerjack looked down at her. His auburn eyes were remarkably gentle and reminded Katie of hot cocoa on cold winter mornings back in Gasthof. "Well, Miss Annie, there's been a heap of trouble along the railway lines."

"Really? Like what?"

Katie watched quietly as her twin sister proceeded to fall for an English cowboy.

"Well," Crackerjack began, "bandits will pile rocks on the rails. When the train derails, they have men waiting to round up the cattle. They steal them, then drive 'em on and sell 'em at market." His natural smile still graced his lips. It looked as though he would explain anything Annie wanted to know, and gladly, however many times she needed to hear it.

"That sounds so dangerous." Annie's eyebrows crept up her forehead. "Could you be hurt?"

Crackerjack ducked his head as his smile transformed into an embarrassed grin. "Well, that's why we're driving them the old fashioned way. A lot easier to fight off a band of rustlers from the back of your horse than from the back of a train car."

Unwilling to be left out of the conversation any longer, Katie asked the question that had been burning on her tongue since the display in the corral. "George—er, Crackerjack— what are you going to call that horse?"

"Hmm?" he asked, still gazing at Annie as though she were a priceless painting.

"Your new horse. The mustang. What are you going to name her?" Katie tried to use the same gentle tones as he had, but failed in keeping the indignation out of her voice.

"I'd be much obliged if you'd name her, Miss Annie. Boys around here, well, the names we come up with aren't fit to be repeated in front a lady."

Annie drummed her fingers on the pasture fence they'd been following. "I like Parker," she said softly.

Katie wrinkled her nose. "Parker? For a girl horse?" *She never could name animals. It was her who named our milk cow Floppy...*

Annie nodded, a familiar twinkle in her eye. "The woman who saved my sister's life was an Indian. Actually, she was the wife of Quanah Parker, the Comanche chief. And your horse is an Indian pony, right?"

Crackerjack nodded, his neck scarlet.

"Well, then it only makes sense to name her Parker, after Quanah's wife. She saved my best friend, my sister, from the grippe."

Feeling foolish and more than a bit selfish, Katie bit her tongue. The threat of tears burned in her throat. "Parker's a fine name, Annie. Thank you."

"Parker it is," Crackerjack agreed. "The name is settled then."

"There you are," Peter said, trotting up behind them. "Nice place you all have here, George," he said, offering a nod to the young cowman.

Annie didn't acknowledge Peter's arrival. "His name may be George," she breathed, "but we can call him Crackerjack."

Peter cut his eyes over to Katie, his brow furrowed. She nodded and shrugged lightly. *Yes, my sister is smitten with an Englishman.*

"Thank ya," Crackerjack answered. "Say, when's your party here planning on rolling out?"

Peter glanced at the sun. "Well, we've watered our horse and ourselves, so I reckon we could go on this afternoon."

Katie noticed Annie's bright smile fade a touch. She shifted her weight and studied the pasture fence.

Crackerjack adjusted his weight, too. "Well, the boys and me, we're not pullin' out till the morning." He glanced at Annie, who tilted her face to catch his eye. "We'll go at first light, to head for Santa Fe. Most all the chores are done, we're just relaxing until it's time to go." He flashed a dimpled smile at the woman who'd commanded all of his attentions since arriving at the Broken O. "Maybe you'd all like to spend the night and start fresh in the morning?"

Peter glanced at the sun, then back toward the north from whence they'd come. "You think that'd go over with Mr. Adams?"

Crackerjack, who had been fiddling with his fingers, stopped and stood straight. "I reckon he wouldn't object. He let you on his land, so that's sayin' somethin'." He pointed off to the north where Peter had looked. "Had some rustlers come in through that far fence line on several occasions. Heard tell he's buryin' anyone else out that way who cuts through his fence." He grinned. "Since that's the way y'all came from, I reckon he made an exception."

Peter shifted his weight. "I reckon he did."

Nervous chills chased down Katie's backbone and clawed at her stomach. Reaching in her dress pocket, she produced the little book of sonnets the snowy-mustached rancher had given her. "He gave me this, too," she added.

Crackerjack's eyes widened. "Well, little lady, that'd make you pert near family. He's never let that little book out of his sight."

The cold chills that had settled in Katie's gut thawed until they were replaced by a familial warmth resonating through her body. *Family already. I knew I would like Texas.*

Crackerjack sobered. "Whenever you do decide to head out, fill your jugs from our well. Don't stop at the next spread and sure as he—" He paused and considered his audience. "Sure as shootin' don't drink from their well. Or cistern."

"Why's that?" Peter and Katie asked in unison before sharing a smile.

Crackerjack pulled his hat down and nodded off to the south. "Fellow that owns that place is called Pappy Simmons. Runs the place with his son and his son-in-law. He's a bad man, Peter. *Muy malo.*" Crackerjack plucked a pinwheel weed from the swaying grass and popped it in his mouth, shaking his head. "He's very bad. Won't go into detail, but suffice it say his son-in-law caught him red-handed and sent a ranch hand into Amarillo with word for the sheriff to come out to the spread and take care of the matter, nice and law-like."

What crimes must he have committed to have been turned on by his own family?

"Well, Pappy Simmons must not have liked the idea of being strung up or something, because he put arsenic in his cistern."

Katie leaned forward. "Why?"

Crackerjack smiled. "Because his son-in-law stopped there for a cool drink every day on his way in from work. He was brandin' cattle out on the back forty." He nodded to Peter and continued. "So Pappy Simmons sat on his porch and watched that cistern, so I've been told. But his son-in-law didn't stop at the cistern that day, just kept on going."

Katie glanced at Annie, who stared at Crackerjack through wide eyes.

"Pappy got disgusted and went inside. Wasn't till some workers came by after dark that they found Pappy's son out there—mostly dead. He'd drunk from the cistern instead."

Annie shivered. "He is a bad man, isn't he? Did his son, well, die?"

Crackerjack shook his head. "Not yet. Rumor is Simmons will be selling his spread soon." Glancing back down to Annie, Crackerjack smiled sweetly. "Just don't go a-drinkin' from his well."

Chapter 13

Broken O Cattle Company Ranch

Crackerjack glanced at Annie as the sun rushed toward the horizon, pausing in its descent to bathe the entire western sky in a heavenly portrait of color. Gazing upon the sunset together, Katie couldn't help but notice how terribly at home Annie looked next to Crackerjack, their forms illuminated by the swirls of pinks, gold, and purples. The sunset itself was so quietly beautiful that a hush fell over the four of them.

Peter was the first to break the churchlike silence. "Yup, that's just about right, right there." No explanation was needed as they stood in solemn awe of the western sky.

"Some folks, I believe you called them the English," Crackerjack began. "Well, they save up all their sinnin' and then go in on Sundays for their churchin' and forgivin' and the like." Crackerjack stared out over the wild, western land. "But not me. I reckon I spend some time with my Maker every day. Every mornin' and every night. Right here, lookin' at all that beauty He creates just for those of us that bother to stop and look."

Annie sighed.

Tearing his gaze from the sunset, Crackerjack looked down at her. "Would you like to see the cattle we're driving, Annie?" he asked softly.

Still unnerved by the horrible story of Pappy Simmons,

Katie stepped quickly to join Peter. Together, they trailed along behind Annie and Crackerjack, careful not to stray too far from the pasture fence. The lowing of the cattle filled the air long before the cattle themselves came into view. Still on the right side of the fence, the four of them topped a small ridge. There below, the cattle spread out before them, filling a small valley. Katie and Annie sucked in a collective, audible gasp.

"Only that little wood fence between us and all of them?" Annie asked. Surprisingly, her voice didn't sound nervous, but excited. "And those horns—oh George," she cooed, too enamored with the moment to use his nickname. "They're some of the most beautiful creatures I've ever seen." Her voice was breathy, something Katie had never before heard.

"They look scary to me," Katie added.

Peter shot her a pained look.

She dropped her voice to a whisper. "I'm sorry Peter, but they do."

Annie stared down at the lowing, grazing beasts. "No, they're simply gorgeous. Just as God created them."

Crackerjack smiled. "Their horns are really something, aren't they? Longhorn cattle are gentle compared to regular cattle too, despite the horns." He glanced at Annie, searching her eyes. "You talk like a real cattlewoman, Annie. Have you been around them before?"

Annie shied away from his deep stare. "A little. Milk cows mostly."

Katie stood on tiptoe and whispered into Peter's shoulder. "We may as well not even be here. If we disappeared into that canyon there," she gestured with her hands, "they'd never even know it."

Reaching down, Peter gave her hand a squeeze. "It is eating away at you, isn't it?"

Katie cocked her head. "What is?"

Peter grinned. "You not being the center of attention for once," he teased.

Katie's mouth fell open.

Flashing a wink, Peter cut her off. "Let's go see that canyon you spotted while we still have some light."

Still chatting about the beauty of Broken O's cattle, Annie and Crackerjack fell in naturally behind Peter and Katie and they walked down to view the canyon that seemed to open up, like a whispered secret in the land that spread out before them. The vastness of it took Katie's breath. "Talk about beautiful," she whispered.

"Almost magical," Crackerjack said. The rays of the sinking sun seemed to collect in the canyon, bouncing back an almost midday glow in parts while others were already overtaken by the blue-black shadows of the night.

Accentuated layers of pinks, oranges, and browns were illuminated in such a way that tears sprang to Katie's eyes. She sniffed them back.

Crackerjack glanced at her, for the first time fully turning his attention from Annie, his face beaming.

"Excuse me," Katie stammered, swiping at her damp cheeks with her palm.

"No excusin' necessary, Miss Katie."

She dipped her head, suddenly embarrassed. "I don't know what's come over me." Emotion surged within her, threatening to drown the very life it belonged to.

"Quite normal when you see your home again," Crackerjack explained, "or see it for the first time. Welcome home,

Miss Katie." Beaming, he turned back to take in the rest of the sunset with Annie. "See what I mean about being spittin' distance from God at times like this?" he whispered to her.

Annie nodded.

Giving over to the enchanted moment, Katie made no more motion to hide or brush away her tears. Instead, she gazed at the canyon and let her heart fill with awe. "Home," she sobbed. "Thank you, God. Thank you."

Peter took her hand in his. When she didn't pull away, he rubbed his thumb along the ridge of her knuckles. She gripped back tightly with her fingers. *We made it. Home.*

When the display was over on the western horizon and twilight was heavy on their shoulders, Peter gave their joined hands a swing. "Welcome home, Katie Knepp."

"Texas. Our home," she whispered. A rogue breeze kicked up, swirling coolness around them. Katie glanced over at her sister, barely visible in the falling darkness. She thought she saw Crackerjack offer her his arm.

Suddenly, the young cowman spoke. "I'll lead you folks back to the bunkhouse by moonlight," he said. "Be mindful of rattlers, now."

Katie shivered. *Rattlers?* Stepping quickly, she and Peter fell in behind them.

The silvery rays of the rising moon proved Katie's theory right. Annie's arm was linked with that of the gentlemanly Texas cowman, George "Crackerjack" Guthrie.

They could hear the music long before they reached the bunkhouses. Crackerjack perked up. "Hear that bunkhouse bass? The boys are lettin' loose a bit before we leave out in the morning."

"Crackerjack," Jim called, halting his puffing into a harmonica as they approached the welcoming glow of the open campfire. "Saved you and your new friends a plate of bar-be-cue." With a wave, Jim turned his attention from his brother back to his harmonica.

Crackerjack led them to a long wooden picnic table where four dented tin plates sat, filled and waiting. A tall, silver-haired woman strode out from a shadowy recess between the bunkhouses, "Dinner is served," she announced taking a seat on the splintery bench. "I hope you don't mind if Cabe and I join you for dinner?"

Katie grinned and stuck out her hand to the older woman with the sapphire-blue eyes. "You must be Marge! We were supposed to ask you to save a plate for your husband."

Marge took it and mirrored Katie's smile.

Though thin, Katie was quite sure given the sinewy muscles in Marge's arms, she probably could have matched any one of the dancing cowboys at daily chores, then go on to prepare the day's meals, all without breaking a sweat. A certain warmth exuded from the blue-eyed woman with the silver topknot, giving Katie a feeling as though she'd known her for years. *She could be an Amish woman just as easily as she could be English.*

Cabe's deep laugh came from the same dark recess, punctuating the moment. A second later, he appeared with a tin of biscuits. "I don't like to cook my biscuits out in the open where my oven might get kicked over," he explained, taking a seat next to his wife.

Katie looked at Marge, her head cocked.

Marge patted her husband on the back as he slid down next to her and began to explain. "I have tried my hardest to make biscuits that my Cabe'll enjoy. Oh, don't get me wrong, he'll eat what I cook—" She locked eyes with everyone at the table before turning her attentions back to her snowy-haired husband. "But he simply doesn't like anyone's biscuits but his own. Says he does something with the lard when he adds it…" Marge turned up her hands and shrugged with feigned exasperation.

"It's because I have a secret ingredient," Cabe whispered loudly from behind his hand, obviously teasing his wife.

Peter nudged Katie and tilted his lips into a smile. He didn't say it, but Katie could almost hear his thoughts. *That could be us someday.*

"So I tell him," Marge continued, "if you're gonna fuss and flit around like a vulture at a necktie party that's runnin' late, then you may as well just make your biscuits yourself." She nodded as if to seal the subject to further discussion. "And he has every day for 22 years.

"And my Marge always has me a little campfire built off away from everyone else and my Dutch oven heating up for when I get in, just so I can make my biscuits in peace." The gunfighter smiled tenderly at his sweetheart.

"I can't wait to taste one," Katie declared, shattering the moment. "I think I'll need a drink first though."

A small bucket of water sat in the middle of the table. "Round here we drink right from the dipper," Crackerjack explained when he noticed Annie searching the table. "If that's bothersome, I'll rustle us up some cups. Gotta be one around here somewhere." He rose partway from the seat.

Annie waved one delicate hand. "No, we're in Texas now.

I will follow your lead." Reaching out her hand to him, they clasped over the table. "Would you like to lead us in a prayer to give thanks for this food, Crackerjack?"

Katie bit back another smile and took her sister's hand. Peter, George, Marge, and Cabe linked hands as Annie offered a moonlit smile to Crackerjack.

"I'd be honored," he croaked.

Clearing his throat and breaking his grasp with Peter only long enough to swipe off his hat, Crackerjack began. "Father, thank you for these cattle which are my livelihood and for our guests here at the Broken O."

Katie peeked at Crackerjack, whose eyes were closed. "Please bless them on their journey into the country that You made special for people with hearts like ours." Crackerjack's eyebrows knitted together over his closed eyes as he continued. "Please continue to pour out Your blessings on those who follow Your word, and bless my future family and future ranch—if it be in Your will to bless me with those things at all. Um, Amen."

Before they could loosen their hands, Annie did the unthinkable. "God," she began, her eyes still shut fast, "please don't forget Your children as they leave on a journey for Santa Fe. Please bless them and let them come to know You better. In Jesus' name I pray. Amen."

Katie saw Crackerjack give Annie's fingers a little squeeze. "Amen," he said again, his voice full of reverence.

Before anyone could release their hands, Cabe spoke up. "And this, our life, exempt from public haunt, finds tongues in trees, books in the running brooks, sermons in stones, and good in everything. Amen."

Peter's stomach rumbled loudly, prompting a giggle from

the entire table. Behind them, the ranch hands partied on to the tune of fiddles, Jim's harmonica, and that thumping bunkhouse bass, made from an overturned washtub. One cowboy even was clinking together a pair of spoons.

"Katie, after we eat, can I—er, *may* I—have a dance?" Peter's eyes were tender as he gauged her response.

Again, her mouth fell open. She glanced at her sister, knowing full well that such a request would have been unheard of back in Gasthof. Some fragments of a truism found their way to the forefront of her swirling mind. Something about Rome, Romans, and being in Rome. Following on the tail of the truism, was a piece of scripture from Ecclesiastes she'd memorized long ago. *To everything there is a season, and a time to every purpose under the heaven.* Her mind skimmed the rest of the scripture verse. *A time to be born, die, plant, pluck up what was planted... a time to kill, heal, break down, build up... weep, laugh mourn.* Katie chewed harder and looked out over the jolly cowboys as they each took turns showing off their dancing moves in the soft glow of the cheery fire. *And a time to dance.*

Turning her attention back to Peter, she swallowed down the mashed potatoes. "Yes, Peter Wagler. I would be honored to dance with you tonight."

Never before had Katie felt so at war with herself—or at peace—than when she stepped out into that open, dusty space, lit only by firelight, with Peter by her side. As soon as they stepped gingerly out onto the makeshift dance floor, the cowboy on the fiddle slowed his sawing and the unseen Jim playing the harmonica dropped his notes until they sang out in the still night air, long and low. Katie shivered as Peter faced her, looking more handsome bathed in moonlight than he did during the daytime.

"Well—" Katie began, but Peter shushed her.

With his lips tilted into a beautiful smile, he took her hand. "No words," he whispered as he pulled her next to him. With his strong arms around her, she'd never felt so safe. Or so vulnerable.

She inhaled his scent as the music played on and they swayed slowly together to the tune. Katie closed her eyes and a cowboy began to sing.

"Price your happiness, blessed Saxony.
Because God is given the throne of thy king.
Happy land."

Holding him close with his arms wrapped around her, Katie knew. She simply knew. Her prayer had been answered and she was where she was meant to be. She was with the man she was meant to be with, her Peter. "Peter, I—"

Lifting an arm from around her waist, Peter brushed her lips with one callused finger. "Hush, Katie girl. We have all the time in the world to talk, but our first dance only happens once."

Katie's lips spread into an aching smile. Closing her eyes again, she rested her cheek on his chest and swayed to the tune. Given the noise from behind her, Annie had apparently accepted a dance from Crackerjack. Unlike her and Peter, Annie and Crackerjack were chattering nonstop.

"I hope to have my own ranch someday," Crackerjack said.

Annie's voice replied softly. "Such a noble dream. After seeing those longhorns, I understand why. Did your father ranch before you?"

"Pa was a doc back in Philadelphia. I went to all the good schools, learned all the good lessons. But I didn't want that life."

"What did—do—you want?"

Katie dared a peek over her shoulder at her sister who, since meeting the handsome young bronc-bustin' Crackerjack, had become quite brazen. Annie stared at her dance partner dreamily, as though seeing a man for the first time. *Your sister is in love, Katie Knepp. Just like you, your sister is in love.*

"I wanted adventure," Crackerjack answered, staring down into Katie's eyes just as dreamily. "So I wound up here, where Mr. Adams took me in. Been here a few years now." Lifting a hand, he fingered one of her covering strings. "Now, let's talk about you."

Their swaying took them out of earshot, but it didn't matter. Katie exhaled, secure in the knowledge that all of them; her sister, her Peter, and herself—and most likely a feisty young cowman named Crackerjack—had found themselves in the glow of a Texas campfire, just before a cattle drive to Santa Fe.

Chapter 14

Old Amarillo

The next morning dawned much too early, with the sun's gentle morning rays peeking through the dirty oil-paper that was stretched taut over the bunkhouse window. *I suppose that's just there to keep out the dust*, Katie figured. It certainly does nothing to keep out the sunshine. She rolled over and propped her head up on her hand. *Well, most of the dust.* Snug beneath her quilt, Katie lay on the cot and watched the dust motes dance their own dance in the scattered beams. She sighed, the memory of Peter's arms still fresh and sweet in her mind.

In the next cot, Annie sat up straight as a pin, suddenly very awake. "Did we miss it," she asked. Throwing her legs over the side of her bunk, she threw on the dress she'd laid out the night before. "Have Crackerjack and the other cowmen already left on the trail?"

Suddenly awake herself, Katie sprang up and peeked out the door. "They're just mounting up. Here," she dashed to her sister's side. "Let me help you with your covering."

When Katie and Annie burst from the bunkhouse door, Peter already had the buggy hitched and ready. "Good morning, Knepp ladies. Sleeping late this morning?"

Katie offered a bright smile. "Good morning, Texan." Somehow, the magic of the night before had carried over into the morning sunlight, much the same way as those dreamlike nights at a Gasthof Village barn raising had.

Nearby, Crackerjack sat atop Parker, his still-skittish mustang. With that trademark, and somewhat strangely familiar, grin, he tipped his hat with one finger. Without any words, Annie strode over to tell her Texas cowboy goodbye.

Katie joined Peter at the buggy to watch Annie and Crackerjack's goodbye.

"I'll send word from Santa Fe to let you know we made it safe, if you like."

Annie nodded beneath her crooked covering. Katie thought she heard a sniffle.

Parker stomped sideways and swished her tail, obviously ready to do something other than just stand there. Reaching down, Crackerjack stroked Annie's cheek with a finger. "Wasn't lookin' for no woman when you come along, Annie Knepp. But believe this old Philadelphia boy when I tell you that my eyes are closed to women until you walk into my life again."

Oh my, Katie thought, drawing her fist to her mouth. She sniffed back a tear.

With a sly wink, George "Crackerjack" Guthrie turned Parker's head and galloped off to join the other boys as they gathered the massive herd of Texas longhorn cattle.

"Goodbye, George Guthrie," Annie whispered to his retreating back. A soft wind whispered around them, blowing Annie's covering strings back over her shoulder. Lifting a finger, she swiped at a tear. "Goodbye."

Katie noticed right off the familiar stirring in Annie's eyes as they drove off the Broken O. "You really are quite smitten with Crackerjack, aren't you Annie?" It was obvious Katie was delighting in her sister's crush. "Tell me everything. I saw you dance with him." Katie was turned completely around on the buggy seat, facing her sister. "Did you bond with him? Oh, who am I kidding, of course you did." Katie sucked in her bottom lip while the questions formed, one after another, in her mind. Chewing, she considered each question only for a moment before flinging it at her sister. "Does he love God, Annie? I mean, like we do?"

Annie waited for Katie to take a breath before she broke in. "Yes. I didn't bond with him, I fell in love with him, but only after I knew that he had fallen in love with *me*." Talking about love brought a crimson tint to Annie's cheeks. "There is just something so special about him."

Katie sighed. "Isn't it wonderful?" She shifted on the seat and looked at Peter.

"Thanks for including me in your conversation," Peter teased. "With all this talk of love, I feel it's only right to let you ladies in on a little secret. I spoke to Crackerjack Guthrie this morning, myself."

Katie and Annie shared a silly look, then a giggle.

Unfazed, Peter continued. "Annie? He said he knew he loved you the moment you rode onto the Broken O." Peter lifted himself off the wagon seat and pulled something from his pocket.

Both girls fell silent.

"He also said if you loved him, the way God intended for woman to love a man, than I was to give you this." Keeping his eyes on the narrow trail, he handed the treasure over his shoulder to Annie.

Katie gasped. "Is that real gold?"

"It's his pa's gold pocket watch."

With a hiccup, Annie began to cry.

Peter softened his voice. "Said he'll be just a telegram away and he would love to know your feelings for him for himself." Peter smiled. "Guess all English ain't so bad after all, are they?"

"Glad we stocked up on water," Peter mused. "That decrepit place there is the Simmons spread."

Katie glanced at the dilapidated ranch. "Looks like the Simmons' family has already pulled up stakes and moved on." The front door of the main house swung, forgotten and broken, in the hot breeze. "I wonder if his son died?"

Annie pointed from the back of the buggy. "Not sure who that belongs to, but someone's buried there." A lone white cross, laid over on its side, marked someone's final resting place in the front yard of the Simmons' place.

Katie shivered as Peter snapped the reins over Sookie's back. No doubt he felt the same haunting darkness that seemed to loom over the Simmons' empty home site as she did. With Sookie's quick clip, they passed the vacant property quickly.

When the eerie feeling had passed, Peter wiped his sleeve across his forehead. "Didn't figure it to get so hot so early on in the day."

Katie adjusted her dress and slouched back against the faded buggy seat. She flicked her covering strings and tried to think about anything but the encroaching heat. Indeed, as magical as the night before had been, those sweet and hazy memories faded as the temperature rose. All she wanted to do was go jump in a cool creek and preferably nap under a shady tree somewhere.

"Amarillo Creek."

Katie sat up. "What did you say, Annie?"

Annie pointed. "That little sign. Right there, look!"

Peter snapped the reins over Sookie's back again. "There it is. Amarillo Creek."

Maybe they'll let me dip my toes in just for a moment. Katie peeked out of the buggy window as they drove over the ramshackle little bridge. "Peter!" Her jaw went slack as she turned to face him. "There's no water in that creek."

Peter bobbed his head. "I was afraid of that. At least we're close to the Mennonite settlement. Didn't you say it was just outside of Amarillo, Katie?"

Searching her memory for the exact location as to where the settlement was located, Katie scanned the wooded horizon. *I never got the exact location.* She bit her bottom lip and willed the knots to untie in her stomach. *How stupid of me to think we'd just stumble on it, or drive right to it...*

Annie and Peter waited for her to answer. "Katie?"

God, help me. How do I tell Peter and Annie I brought them out into the Texas wilderness without even knowing where I was going? Then, her eyes focused on another small, immaculately printed sign. "Look!" Katie sprang out of her seat, almost flipping forward out of the buggy. "A honey stand," she shrieked. "Look at the name on the sign, the name!"

Peter squinted and Annie leaned forward. "Joseph..." Peter tried. "That's all I can make out. Can you read it, Annie?"

"Um, maybe if we get a bit closer."

Katie tilted her chin. "You'll find it says, Goetz." *Finally, I read something they couldn't.* Crossing her arms, Katie sat back against the seat. *Or maybe my eyes are just better at reading Mennonite names long distances.*

Peter reined Sookie to a halt. "You're right Katie. Joseph Goetz. And look at this." He hopped out of the buggy and trotted around behind them. "They're selling their honey on the honor system. Just like we do, er, well, how *they* do back at Gasthof."

Leaning over, Katie and Annie watched as Peter lifted a jar of the thick amber liquid. Filled to above the lid line, the honey hardly moved as Peter turned the jar first this way and then back that way, examining the contents. It looked deliciously sweet. Katie licked her lips. Setting the jar back down with the others, Peter plucked up the rock which held down the cash money paid out by passersby in exchange for a jar of Mennonite Texas honey.

"Joseph Goetz hasn't done too badly," Peter mused, counting out the cash. "He's made five dollars." He glanced up at the girls and shoved the money into his pocket. "Let's take it to him, shall we?"

Katie and Annie squealed. *The end is in sight*, Katie thought as they drove down the trail. *I never thought I would be glad for an adventure to be over, but goodness, I am glad.* She perked up as Sookie turned through a whitewashed fence. The house was visible at the end of the fence line.

Katie turned to Annie, her heart thumping louder now than it had back at Robber's Roost. "Sister, we're here." She grasped Annie's hand over the buggy seat.

Annie's voice came out in a whisper. "I know. I'm so glad I came. Couldn't have stood being without my sister and best friend."

Katie tightened her lips stoically. "And you wouldn't have

gotten to meet Crackerjack Guthrie, best mustang-breaker in Texas." Loosening her face, Katie gave over to a spate of laughter.

"Yes, that too," Annie agreed, her ears bright red.

Katie steeled her backbone. Sensing eyes upon her, she swiveled slowly on the buggy seat. Sure enough, an older man and his entire family had appeared in their yard. There they stood, together as a family, watching and waiting for the approaching buggy as it drove up the path to their home.

Katie's mind began to swirl with insecurities. Slapping her sweaty hand over Peter's, she watched the world go fuzzy before her eyes. "I feel a might faint," she whispered, managing a swallow. Reaching up with her other clammy hand, she tugged at the high collar of her dress. *It's choking me*, she thought wildly. Deep in her chest, her heart quickened to a thunderous beat.

"Katie?" Annie's worried voice floated over the buggy seat. Still, it sounded very far away. "Peter, is she alright?"

Katie gasped, trying to get the air that surrounded her to follow through to her lungs. "We should have done something," she rasped, still pulling at her collar. Deftly, Annie unbuttoned the top hook-and-eye button. *Finally, I can breathe.* "I don't know if we're welcome. I should have sent a telegram."

Peter stopped the buggy. His hands were on her face in an instant, petting and holding. "Katie, calm down."

She stared at him, his outline fuzzy, as she writhed on the buggy seat. Her mind raced this way and that and all at once, the world was closing in on her. "Turn around. Let's go home."

Annie peeked over the buggy seat. "You mean to tell me you've come all this way? Braving our first family, the

Ordnung, the grippe, a poetry-wielding gunslinger, and a Texan so crazy in his head that he shot a man, then gave his widow his entire life's work—his ranch?" Annie clicked her tongue against her teeth as Katie's breathing started to slow.

"Don't forget the hydrophobia," Peter added, addressing Annie. "She did want to pet the rabid bobcat, you know."

Annie patted her sister's shoulder and talked over her head. "And outlaws? Weren't there outlaws?"

"Several outlaws actually. Outlaws of all kinds." Peter smiled down at Katie's sweat-laced, upturned face. "She even showed one the way to the Lord."

Annie still patted and rubbed. "Wasn't there a fire along the way?"

"A bad fire," Peter agreed. "What was it Crackerjack said? *Muy malo?*"

Annie flushed.

"And the coyotes." Katie's voice was a dry whisper. "The first night, the coyotes tried to eat my venison steak dinner. I flung it at them and ran."

Annie and Peter shared in a quiet chuckle. "See there now," Annie cooed, smoothing at the parts of Katie's dress that she could reach. "See there? Come all that way. Through all those obstacles, unafraid?" She reached and slid Katie's neck button back into place. Then, she sat back, signaling to Peter that she was ready to go. "Only to be scared now that we're at the tail end of our journey? Not my sister. Not the fearless Katie Knepp." Annie dropped her voice to a joshing whisper. "Or Katie Wagler."

"On that note," Peter said, turning his attention back to the front. "Let's go meet the Goetz's."

Katie still felt weak and trembly. "But they're not expecting us Peter; their like to think we're as mad as that bobcat." Slowly, she pushed herself up on the seat and forced herself to breathe. *The world is not folding in on me. The world is not folding in on me...*

"They look to be expecting us," Peter countered.

Katie tried not to stare as she examined the family. There was Joseph, obviously then she could pick out his wife. When she started to count the kids, however, she got confused and came up with ten. *Surely that's not right, is it?* "But how could they be expecting us?"

Peter tilted his chin into the air. "Sarah Wagler taught me to be a gracious guest. Always send word before going somewhere. If the place you're going happens to be in Texas, well, the appropriate thing to do is to send a telegram." His full lips pulled back, revealing two rows of perfectly straight, perfectly white teeth. "I sent it myself from Montgomery, figured you forgot."

Katie exhaled. "Thank you, Peter." *Thank you again, God. For well, You know, everything.*

"Faith of a mustard seed," Peter sang quietly in a melodic voice. He reined Sookie to a halt in front of the Goetz's barn. The Mennonite family, smiling and waving, circled around to greet them.

"*Hallo* and *wilkommen*," Joseph said, grinning and extending his hand to Peter. A robust man just a smidge older than her father, he looked as though he might break out into a jolly dance at any moment.

Peter shook his hand. "*Hallo* and thanks for the—" Before Peter could finish, Joseph pulled him right out of the buggy and into a bear-like hug. "Welcome to Texas and to our home and settlement. We thank God you made the trip safely and could join us."

A small smile teased the corners of Katie's lips as she watched the display. *Yes, colorful characters in Texas, for sure.*

Catching her watching, Joseph cocked his head to the side and grinned. "Ah, you must be Katie. Katie Knepp. Come here Katie, welcome!" Holding out his arms, Joseph Goetz helped her from the buggy and greeted her with a slightly crushing hug.

Releasing her, Joseph glanced into the wagon. Spying Annie, he grinned and cocked his head. "And who have we here?"

"I'm Annie, Katie's sister. I caught up and surprised them on the way here." Annie's voice was as meek as it had been since before meeting Crackerjack.

Joseph laughed a deep, rumbling laugh that seemed to fill the entire expanse of the deep blue Texas sky. "Come here Annie Knepp. You are family, too." Helping her out, Joseph greeted blushing Annie with the same brand of bearlike hug as he had both Katie and Peter.

Katie watched in amazement. She could feel the silly grin on her face, but made no motion to hide it. *How nice of him to call us family.*

Resting his beefy hands on his protruding belly, Joseph continued in contented tones. "Now Katie, Annie, Peter. Please allow me to introduce you to my family." Turning, he gestured widely with his arm. "Here we have Barbara, my wife."

Stepping forward, Barbara greeted Peter with a hug.

"Annie," Katie mouthed. "Does this woman look familiar to you, too?"

Craning her neck, Annie and Katie watched as Barbara smiled and chatted with Peter. "Yes, it's something about her eyes," Annie agreed quietly.

Katie studied Barbara's smiling eyes. She was a bit older than her mother Katherine, but when she smiled, there was something about the way the creases folded around her eyes that caught Katie's attention. *Something wise...*

Stepping to Katie, Barbara pulled her into a tight embrace. "I prayed for you every night, Katie. So did the children," she whispered softly in their shared Pennsylvania Dutch. "We're so blessed to have you with us. Since we learned of your prayer to come to Texas, it's been all the talk about the Goetz home." Releasing from the warm hug, Katie noticed the dampness which had streaked down Barbara's kindly face.

"Thank you," Katie managed in their native tongue. "It's so good to see another woman in a covering." *Does my first language now have a twang?* "Well, besides my sister."

"When Peter sent the telegram and told us you were coming, you answered a prayer of mine, Katie." Reaching out her hand, Barbara clasped Annie's and in hers and pulled her up to join them. "You too, Annie. Let me tell you girls a story. My mother's name was Maria Sybilla Steheli."

Katie nodded, not sure where Barbara was going with the story. "That's a beautiful name. Is it German?"

"Yes, it is." Barbara paused before continuing, ensuring she had their full attention. "Katie, Annie. My mother Maria was your mother's eldest sister by 20 years."

Katie and Annie exchanged a baffled look. "That explains why she looks so much like Ma," Katie blurted out before she could stop herself.

Barbara's eyes twinkled. "Back in Germany, my mother, Maria, left on Rumspringa and never came home. The family shunned her, as per their accepted customs.

"Ordnung! The accepted customs." Katie stared at Annie.

"*That's* why Ma and Pa said that about putting family before Ordnung, with their coming south to join us," Annie whispered.

Fresh tears welled in Barbara's eyes. "We will be a family rejoined, we will." Composing herself, she continued with the story of their lineage. "Well, like you girls, Maria didn't want to leave her heritage. She married a Mennonite man, Mario Steheli."

My family. A long, lost branch of my family—I found them because I came to Texas. Tears welled in Katie's eyes and she made no motion to stem their flow. Now was most certainly the time for happy tears.

"Mario and Maria came to the United States together and lived out their lives in Lancaster County, Pennsylvania." Barbara opened her arms wide to her great-nieces. "Welcome to the family you may well have never known, had you not inherited my mother's courageous spirit and come south on a prayer."

Katie and Annie were enveloped in Barbara's familiar, beefy hug again. "I'm so glad you're here, girls. Like I said, your coming is an answer to a prayer."

Loudly so as to be heard, Joseph spoke. "Shall we introduce the children now, Mama?"

Turning to her husband but not releasing Katie or Annie, a smiling and sobbing Barbara nodded. "Okay, Papa."

Beaming, Joseph gestured to the throng of children that spread out behind them. "Here we have David, the oldest boy, and oldest child of the Goetz lot. Then comes Mahalia, our oldest daughter, and her sister Sevilla—"

"Named after her grandmother," Katie mused quietly. Barbara squeezed her hand.

As Joseph introduced them, each grinning child stepped forward and welcomed Peter, then Katie, then Annie with a warm hug and a whisper of good will. "Here's little George, and Nancy, and Hannah, and Isaac, wait, we forgot somebody. Jacob. Jacob? Where are you son?"

Glancing about, they spotted Jacob at the edge of the group. With his shoes off and britches rolled up, young Jacob was ankle deep in a mud puddle. Caught in the act while no doubt trying to remain inconspicuous, Jacob's cheeks spread into a wide smile.

"Jacob!" Barbara admonished, releasing the girls and adjusting her covering the same way Katie's own ma would do when she got heated.

Grinning, the youngster simply offered a little, awkward wave. It appeared he feared more getting his britches dirty than being caught ankle-deep in a mud puddle. "Sissy made me a mud puddle Pa. I'm sorry, but I just couldn't wait to play in it. My feet get so *hot* in those shoes." Suddenly remembering himself, he recited his practiced welcome speech. "Welcome, Miss Katie. Welcome, Mister Peter. I pray your trip was fine." Seeing Annie, little Jacob tacked on an impromptu ending. "And welcome to you too, Miss Katie's friend."

A boy after my own heart. Katie grinned at her little cousin and waved as a cheerful giggle rippled through the Goetz's. Joseph turned back to them and sucked in a deep breath. "Now, where was I? Oh yes. And this is our youngest daughter, Elizabeth, and the baby, James."

I was right, there are ten children. Ten little cousins.

Barbara broke the gentle silence. "Now come in and get settled you two. It looks like you could use a cool drink. Springhouse is in the back."

The sun was just beginning its nightly show of splendor when Katie was finally able to venture out of the house again. The bubbly chatter from the young girls, anxious to know everything about everything and as soon as possible, had kept Katie's head in a constant state of whirling since arriving at the Goetz's. Wonderful, wonderful whirling. She glanced about the wide open yard. *Peter has to be here somewhere.*

"Perhaps you and Peter will have a family this large someday," Annie had whispered teasingly as they passed one another amid the bustle of the Goetz house.

Not if I can't find him, Katie thought with a smile.

Joseph's voice boomed from the side of the house. "The Topeka–Santa Fe railroad runs that-a-way, and the Fort Worth–Denver City line runs that-a-way." As Katie rounded the corner of the house, Joseph looked a little bit like a confused scarecrow, with his arms akimbo.

Katie let go of the tension of the trail and welcomed the wide smile that pushed her cheeks back into an ache. *Maybe someday Peter and I will have a large, wonderful family like the Goetz's. But first—* Gathering her skirt in her hand and all of the wits she could muster, she marched out into the setting sun to join the men.

They had made it, they were in Texas. They were at the Goetz's house. They weren't going to get any more *here* than they already were. The time had come for her to tell Peter that she loved him.

"482 people in town you say," Peter mused. His arms were crossed and his chin rested on his palm thoughtfully. "That's a hefty sum of folks."

Joseph nodded in agreement, mirroring Peter's stance. "Oh, Amarillo is growing alright. Business is booming everywhere—" His voice trailed off into the nightly masterpiece in the sky. "What will you be doing for business, Peter? You are welcome to join us in making honey."

Remembering the honey stand, Peter reached into his pocket. "Here, cash money from your stand by Amarillo Creek." Shifting slightly, he welcomed Katie into their conversation with a wave and a beckon. "Did you grab the rest of Mr. Goetz's honey jars, Katie?"

Stepping to join them, Katie nodded. "Yes, well Annie did. We've already given them to Mrs. Goetz." She grinned. "My great-aunt. But I suppose you already know that."

Joseph Goetz's face transformed from jocular to one unimaginably stoic. He hardly looked like the same happy-go-lucky man at all. Katie scooted a bit closer to Peter and tried to steel her backbone, which threatened to melt like butter under Joseph's hard stare.

Joseph looked first at Peter, then at Katie. "Now see here," he began, his voice heavy. "Let us all get one thing straight right now."

I knew you shouldn't have grabbed that money, Peter, Katie thought as loudly as she could. *We should have just left it be.*

Keeping up his hard look at the both of them, Joseph spoke in his usual *forte* voice. "I am *Uncle Joseph* and my wife is *Aunt Barbara.* We welcomed you all into our family. You *are* family. No more of this Mister Goetz and Missus Goetz business." As quickly as it had gone stoic, his full face softened again and he let go a raucous belly laugh.

Peter and Katie joined in, their laughter filling the plains as the perfect accompaniment to the glorious pastel streaks of the setting sun. When the moment passed, Peter picked up the conversation where they'd left off. "I thank you kindly, Uncle Joseph. You asked what I had planned for business. I had planned to start a furniture store, if that's a marketable trade in Oneida, er, Amarillo."

"Oneida? You don't hear it called that but by the old timers anymore." Joseph shook his head nostalgically. "You planned ahead. I knew I liked you. But to answer your question, yes. There is a market for furniture. No Amish folks here to make the hand-hewn old-world goods. The public will be ready to buy." He turned his smiling attentions to Katie. "And I bet you sew, don't you, Katie girl?"

Katie nodded. "I do, so does my sister. However, I'd like to help Peter with the furniture as much as I can. Sewing in the evening relaxes me, much more than doing it during the day." *There it is again, that brutal honesty.* Katie could almost hear her mother's admonishment in her mind.

Joseph rubbed his chin. "Katie girl, I wouldn't expect anything less from a woman who travels across some of the wildest country in America on nothing but a prayer. My blessing is on you both. Stay at the Goetz house as long as you need."

Katie grinned. Before she could help it, she found herself giving a bear-like hug to her uncle, Joseph Goetz.

Laughing, Joseph thumped her on the back with one brawny hand. "Amarillo's up to 14 saloons and 11 gambling houses."

Backing away, Katie felt her jaw go slack. "That many English places to drink and gamble?"

Joseph nodded, gazing off into the distance toward the sprawling metropolis formerly known as Oneida. One hand absently stroked his modest beard as he thought. "Oh, and they're up to two schools now, too."

Chapter 15

Old Amarillo

"**I** think, no, I *know*, Rockwood is the perfect name, Peter." Katie examined the shingle as Peter nailed it to the eave of their little, borrowed house. "But do you think that your parents will like the name? After all, this is yours and your father's furniture store." She flashed her beau a grin.

"We leaned on The Rock all the way down here." Peter grinned. "Now, we can make some stuff out of wood for Him. Pa'll love it." Extending his hand to Katie, they stepped to admire their handiwork.

A flash of movement caught Katie's eye. It only took a moment for the Texan's build to register with her, even though this time, he was on horseback. "J.B. Smith," Katie exclaimed. "Looks like he's still *Just Bull* to me!" Lifting an arm, she waved wildly.

Trotting in on his tall horse from the dusty trail, Katie could see Bull's smile, wide and sincere, just as it had been the last time they'd met. "Welcome to Texas, Katie Knepp." J.B. swung down from his horse and extended a hand to Peter, all in one fluid motion. "Howdy Mister, I'm J.B. Smith. But you can call me Bull."

Peter mirrored the likable Texan's smile. "Many thanks to you, Bull. I understand Katie's meeting you was the inspiration for this trip."

Bull ducked his head and adjusted his stance on the dirt clods of the Goetz farm. "Is that so?" He glanced up to Katie. "Lil' Sister, you may not have been born south of the Red River, but you have a Texan's soul. I could tell right off. Glad you made it home, lil' darlin'."

Fiddling with her dress pocket, Katie worked hard to contain her excitement. "What brings you out, Mr. Smith?"

Bull's blue eyes sparkled. "How well are you reading nowadays, Katie?"

She flushed. "I've improved over the course of the trip, I believe. Why?"

Three pieces of yellow paper fluttered in Bull's front shirt pocket. Taking them out along with a pair of wire-rimmed spectacles, he examined the telegram papers. Selecting one, he held it out to her. "Here you go, try your eyes at this one."

Shifting his attention back to Peter, Bull spoke like the two were old friends. "Joseph Goetz told me of you guys setting up housekeeping here on his spread, so when I was in town getting my messages I took the liberty of picking up yours, too."

Peter nodded. "Thank you kindly. How was Amarillo?"

"Growing faster than anyone figured. Up to 482 people in town." Bull shook his head. "Founders of this place said we'd do good to set up by the Fort Worth–Denver City railroad, but no one figured on the population explosion, what with the Topeka–Santa Fe line crossing right in the middle of town too."

Peter looked at Katie as she puzzled over the telegram. "I suppose we're some of those folks raising the population, though we didn't come for the cattle business that uses the railroad." Peter gestured over his shoulder to the shingle.

"My parents are going to be joining us soon and Rockwood Furniture will be our mark."

Bull grinned. "Goetz told me that, too. Lots of businesses springing up. Shipping in furniture from the east is expensive. So, like I said, since I was already in town, I talked to a few friends."

Katie took a break from deciphering the thin telegram and ventured a peek at wide-eyed Peter, her ear for news tweaked. "Oh?"

Bull nodded. "Just so happens that several of the 200 new businesses that have gone up so far this year would *love* to carry your authentic, handmade Amish furniture. Exclusive like."

Katie smiled. *Even I know what that means.*

It was Peter's turn to puzzle. "Several? Exclusive?"

"Yes, sir. You can sell to the highest bidder. Cash money will get you through this drought till your crops come in." Bull examined the sky. "Or you can make a deal and sell to all of 'em, whatever you want to do. But the opportunity's there, you just got to go grab it."

There was no hiding Peter's gratitude. Grabbing Bull's thickset hand, he shook hard. "Oh thank you, Mr. Bull. Thank you! Katie? Did you hear?" Turning from the Amarillo cowman, Peter held out his arms.

In a rush of Texas attitude, Katie dashed forward and flung herself into Peter's arms. He spun her around twice before setting her down. "I did! Oh, Peter, we're going to make it down here just fine." Resisting the urge to press her lips to his, Katie forced her attention to return to Bull.

"Well now, will you two also be in need of a preacher soon? Just so happens I know one in town that owes me a favor."

Katie tried to will the smile not to melt from her face, but she couldn't help it. Her zeal turned to sadness in an instant, drawing down the corners of Bull's mouth, too.

"There are no Amish elders to provide the ceremony," Peter explained. "We hoped to keep as close to traditional Amish as possible."

"Mennonite ceremony maybe?" Bull offered, ever helpful. "You kids don't worry about it, I'll talk to Goetz." He nodded at his own suggestion. "Maybe your pa when he gets here, he can help. Or your father-in-law."

Katie perked up. "Did you say Peter's father… *in-law*?"

The sparkle returned to Bull's blue eyes. "Didn't you read the telegram, Katie Knepp?"

To excited to be embarrassed, Katie shook her head. "Couldn't make it out. Every other word was stop, though."

Remembering his regular business, Bull took the telegram from Katie's fingers. "When I stopped to get my messages, as I told Peter, I brought yours too. Shoot, you folks had more messages waiting there than I did!"

"Annie," Katie called. "Come out here, we've got word from Pa!"

Replacing his spectacles on his nose, Bull steadied the telegram in front of him. A sudden gust of that wild west Texas wind, an occurrence to which Katie was slowly becoming accustomed, made Bull grip the little paper tighter.

"Annie, come on, he's about to read," Katie shrieked.

The older Knepp sister, wiping her floured hands on her apron, dashed out and stood next to Katie.

"First one comes from Montgomery, Indiana," Bull relayed. "Your parents have left Gasthof and will be joining y'all just as soon as they can get here."

Katie squealed. "They're on their way!" Grabbing Annie, the sisters embraced and spun around, their plain dresses flying out in a fan and their gauzy covering strings flipping about in a happy dance. "I hope they're not coming the same way we did, though."

J.B. studied the paper. "It says here they'll be coming by rail. All the way to Amarillo."

The Knepp sisters shared another squeal of relieved glee.

"Next one here," J.B. said, squinting down through the glass lenses at the next yellow telegram paper, "is for you, Katie."

A hush fell over the lot of them as Bull began to read. Annie reached and took Katie's hand.

Bull cleared his throat. "Greetings from the Dawson family, Powder River Ranch, Montana Territory. From Logan, Michaela, and Jake. Says here that they hope to hear word of your safe travels soon and hope you find what you're looking for in Texas. Also, to watch out for coyotes." Bull's eyes widened. "You befriended the *Dawson* family?"

The repressed thought of handsome Logan swirled in her mind. *They are still thinking of me. I wonder if Logan thinks of me, too.*

Peter's voice cut into her churning daydream. "Katie? Are you going to answer Mr. Bull?"

Heat creeping up her neck, Katie sucked in a cleansing breath before trusting her tongue. "They took care of me my first night on what I *hoped* was the trail." Katie giggled nervously, remembering the hungry coyotes.

Admiration cloaked Bull's weathered face. "Heir to a cattle fortune, they are. How interesting you not only made their acquaintance, but befriended them as well."

Katie averted her eyes. If anyone knew how close she had

been to going with them to their Montana ranch—to exploring what might have been with sweet young Logan—guilt swam where moments before had been contentment and pleasure.

Bull shook his head. "There's a postscript here from Michaela Dawson. Says she hopes the guide she hired for you in Elizabethtown got you safely to your destination."

Glancing at Peter, she let him take her other hand. "I'll have to assure her that he did that, and so much more," Katie whispered, pushing the thoughts of Logan away again. *Deep down to the darkest and most remote areas of my mind is where they belong and where they'll stay.* She squeezed Peter's hand and offered a shy smile.

J.B. adjusted his glasses, which had slid considerably down his nose. "And the third message is for you, Annie."

Katie grinned as her sister flushed. "Who is it from?" she asked quietly.

"I bet I know," Katie chided, causing Annie's hue to deepen even further.

"Oh, a certain young man in Santa Fe sends word to you, Annie. Says he hopes you enjoy Old Amarillo. He also hopes you received the gift and can send word soon. Signed here, Crackerjack Guthrie."

A lone tear slid down Annie's cheek. Releasing Peter's hand, Katie reached over and took her sister in her arms. "I'll have to send word back," Annie sobbed into her shoulder. Reaching into her pocket, Annie pulled out the gold pocket watch and held it tenderly, as one might hold an irreplaceable antique heirloom.

Bull grinned and held out the telegrams to Peter, who accepted them with a grin. "You people certainly make some interesting friends."

An echo of thunder rolled ominously across the Llano as Bull readied his horse to mount. As he swung himself up into the saddle, he gave a pointed glance to the ever-darkening sky. "Best take cover folks, looks like this draught might break today."

Joseph Goetz emerged from his house with a Texas-sized wave to Mr. Smith.

"See you, Joe," Bull called, turning his horse's face back toward Old Amarillo.

"See you!" Joseph called in reply, cupping his hands around his mouth to be heard over the wind that had just begun to howl.

"Goodbye," called Annie and Katie in unison. Peter waved, too.

Seizing the opportunity for a teaching moment, Joseph spoke directly to Peter. "Look at the horizon." Sure enough, black clouds were beginning to roll in, fast and low, from the north. "It is now time to go below," he said matter-of-factly.

Peter looked more than a bit puzzled. "Below?"

Stepping over near a sprawling mesquite, Joseph began to crank open a thick wooden door.

Katie glanced at Peter. "It opened right out of the ground."

"Family," Joseph called through his cupped hands. No sooner was the word clear of his mouth, another deafening clap of thunder sounded. Katie shuttered at the lingering echo that seemed to roll on forever. At once, the Goetz family filed out of the house and into the cellar, all ten children in a single-file line behind their mother. *To them, it's as though nothing out of the ordinary is happening. I wonder why the hurry? That storm won't be here for—* Katie's eyes widened as the storm clouds, so far away just moments before, were already rolling upon them.

"Clouds like this often bring twisters." Goetz gestured for them to hurry into the cellar. Peter helped Annie to the stairs. She shoved a paper-wrapped package at Katie. "I forgot to give you this. A gift from Minerva."

Katie looked at the package and back to Annie, who grinned. "It's your wedding dress, in a new style she created just for you. She calls it Gypsy-Amish. She made sure it was blue. I might have helped a bit." Turning, Annie descended the stairs into the cellar behind the Goetz's.

Peter offered his arm to Katie. "Shall we?"

Katie crossed her arms across her chest and tilted her chin. "On one condition."

"Alright..."

Katie gave him a sideways glance, much like a schoolmarm might eye a troublesome class of students. "No interruptions?"

Peter licked his lips. "I promise. No interruptions." He made a motion like he was locking his lips together.

She stepped closer, staring deeply into his spring green eyes. "I love you, Peter Wagler. I always have, and I always will."

Peter stared back at her, silent. Her insides quaked. Sure, he'd professed his love for her several times, but now, to stand silent? Widening her eyes, she cocked her head. "Well?"

Peter pointed to his lips and shrugged his shoulders. Katie rolled her eyes, a smile creeping onto her lips. "Unlock your lips. You can speak now."

Making the joking move to unlock his lips, Peter pretended to throw away the imaginary key. "Ahh, there now. And I love you, Katie Knepp."

"Come on, you two!" Joseph's voice was insistent from down in the cellar. "If a twister comes, it'll carry you plumb back to Indiana!"

With eyebrows raised, Peter offered his arm again. "Miss Knepp?"

Linking her arm through his, Katie weaved their fingers together in a tight grip. When their eyes met, she returned Peter's adoring smile. *Thank you, God, for sending me Peter. And for sending us on this journey to Old Amarillo together.*

"Ready for another adventure, Katie?" His voice was so strong and warm that Katie knew she could take refuge in it for the rest of her days.

"As long as we do our adventuring together." She crinkled her nose at him as the icy rain started to fall.

"Of course." He gave her hand a squeeze as she started down the cellar steps. "Hey, Katie?"

Pausing, she glanced at him over her shoulder. "Yes?"

Reaching with his free hand, Peter fingered her gauzy white covering string. "Welcome to Texas, my love."

Katie's lips spread into a wide grin. "Indeed. I'll be needing my black covering of a married woman soon, I hope." Ignoring the flush that burned in her neck, she stood on her tiptoes and met her fiancé's lips in a fiery kiss. "And *wilkommen* to *our* home, Peter. A New Order and a fresh adventure." Katie paused as another ominous rumble of thunder rolled out of the dark, looming clouds and across the northern plains. "Texas style."

Goetz Homestead

"It's only right to have it here," Annie whispered, looking around the Goetz's home. Celery was everywhere, giving a fully traditional Amish feel to the ceremony. "I am glad you could be here."

"I appreciate the invitation, and I welcomed the chance to get out of cow camp for a while," Crackerjack answered. Dressed in a black suit complete with silk string tie, he sat on the bench which had been pushed against the wall for the outpouring of guests for Katie and Peter's wedding. "But getting to see you is what's made it worth my while, Annie."

The grin on Katie's face, which hadn't been present since arriving in Amarillo, ached in her cheeks as she glanced over her shoulder at her chattering twin. The blue dress Minerva sent her, of course, had fit perfectly. Never had she seen its equal and, according to the note in the package, this was the first dress in her Gypsy-Amish line. The note also said that Minerva hoped she could come for a visit soon and learn more dress-making tips from Amish and Mennonite women. *Looks like there may be more to celebrate soon, to see Minerva again!*

A whisper, soft as summer rain, came from beside her. Her heart skipped and began to flutter, even more than it had been already. "Are you ready to be married off?"

Katie shifted her weight and looked at Peter. Handsome, but in a more regal sort of way, his green eyes glittered. She nodded. "We passed every test, didn't we Peter. I'm so glad you stuck by me, even when I didn't deserve it. Or deserve you."

"Oh, Katie you have always deserved the best I could give you."

Katie sniffed back a tear. "I love you, Peter. Now I can tell you I love you anytime I want to."

Peter leaned over, his breath warm on her ear and rustling in her black silk covering. "I love you, too."

Simon Wagler's voice cut them off. "Are you ready?"

Katie smiled at her soon-to-be father-in-law. *This is it. This is really it. I'm about to become Peter's wife.* With a pinch of luck and a load of prayer, Simon and Sarah Wagler had made it not only in time for the ceremony, but in time for Katie's baptism, too. She glanced over her shoulder again, into the audience. Katherine and Jeremiah Knepp each offered their daughter a tiny wave. *To see my father smile again is worth everything I endured in getting here.*

Next to her parents sat Joseph and Barbara Goetz, cheery and jolly as ever she'd seen them. A few tears shone on their cheeks. Bull stood in the doorway, a piece of celery jokingly tucked into the lapel of his suit jacket. In addition to Annie, all of her newfound female cousins stood with her as she made the transition into married life.

A sweet silence befell the room as Simon hefted the Bible from the podium in front of him. "Can you both confess and believe that God has ordained marriage to be a union between one man and one wife, and do you also have the confidence that you are approaching marriage in accordance with the way you have been taught?" Simon glanced from his son to Katie.

"Yes," they answered in unison, sending a snicker through the solemn, gathered crowd.

This is it. The next great adventure. Katie glanced at Peter. *With the man I love.*

Cabe's Snappy Sourdough Biscuits

1 cup of Marge's sourdough starter

2 cups yeast water (made by cutting up a couple of taters and boiling them in 3 cups of water from the spring, until fork tender). Draw off 2 cups of this water.

2 cups of flour

1 heaping tablespoon of store bought sugar

Mix these together and put in a cupboard until it doubles, just like bread dough

4 cups flour regular flour

1 T white store bought sugar

1 tsp salt

1 tsp baking soda

1 T cold, freshly churned butter, diced

Cabe's secret ingredient was to use a dash of cinnamon in his biscuits

Add your sourdough starter to your flour. Mix in the rest of your dry ingredients, including the cinnamon if you want Cabe's special biscuits, and you'll have formed a dough. Add more flour to get the perfect dough consistency where you live. Sprinkle your diced butter cubes over the dough and pinch or "snap" them into the dough with your fingers. Divide your dough into biscuit sized balls and put them in your Dutch oven or seasoned cast iron skillet. Let them rise for 20 minutes. Bake until golden brown, about 30 minutes.

And now, a sneak peek at

ANNIE'S PLAIN PROMISE

AMISH JOURNEYS ~ BOOK 2

Old Amarillo, Texas

Pulling her gauzy white covering down as far as it would go, Annie carefully looked both ways before venturing across Amarillo's dusty Polk Street. Balancing the armload of mended dresses on her shoulder, she picked her way across the deep ruts and clods, listening for rushing wagons.

"To say this town is growing day by day doesn't do Amarillo justice," she muttered.

A train whistle shrieked, demanding her attention. Beneath the baking Texas sun, Annie watched as the richly dressed cattle barons poured out of the train depot and into the plot of land where the rails that led to Santa Fe crossed those that led to Topeka. *En masse*, they made their way to the towering Amarillo Hotel, smiling and chattering amongst themselves and seemingly oblivious to the stares of the passersby.

Coming to claim their share of the cattle trade, Annie thought as she stepped out of the rutty road and onto the safety of the wooden boardwalk. Bound for Wolfin's Mercantile with the armload of dresses they hired her to mend, Annie nonchalantly glanced at Philip Seewald's storefront. *The beginnings of a jewelry store, so I heard rumor.*

167

Three men in inky black dusters with their hats pulled low stood outside and appeared to be remarkably out of place. They seemed to cast an awful lot of glances toward the whitewashed bank, too. Annie said a quick mental prayer. *And some come to take from those who profit from the cattle business. Please, Father, protect those who come in contact with those men.* Annie studied the ground and tried to ignore the icy chills that chased each other down her spine as she passed in front of the black-clad trio. *Just a few more steps and I'll be safely to Wolfin's.*

Holding her breath until she was clear of the men, Annie exhaled and glanced at the newest business that had sprung up almost overnight. *A post office for true postal mail.* Her mood brightened. *To receive letters handwritten by those you love.* A smile found its way onto her lips. *Maybe I'll pen a letter to Crackerjack after I return these dresses and post it to Santa Fe. Surely there's a post office in Santa Fe...*

Popping shots echoed from behind her, shocking Annie from her daydream of handsome George "Crackerjack" Guthrie, the Texas cowman who'd stolen her heart only months before. Ducking into Wolfin's, she dared a peek out from the glass window into the freshly deserted Polk Street. The bank president stood in front of the fancy First National sign, the giant clock behind him ticking down the minutes until ten a.m. and both barrels of his shotgun still smoking. Two of the outlaws writhed in the dusty street, moaning. The third was nowhere that Annie could see.

"You and those dresses made it just in time, judging by the commotion out in the street," Mr. Wolfin said from behind her. "Here, let me help you pick these up so I can pay you, and you can be on your way."

Annie's heart thundered in her chest as she turned to face the mercantile owner. "Yes, just in time," she agreed. A chill coursed through her body when she thought of stepping back out into the street when her business at the mercantile was complete.

Cash money from her mending job jingled in her dress pocket as Annie dashed across the eerily quiet and strangely empty street.

Perhaps I could make it to the post office to send that letter, so I don't have to come back into town later. As she drew nearer to the new post office building, an arm reached out and grabbed her from the shadowed alleyway.

Thoughts of the thwarted third bank bandit burst into her mind. "Help!" Annie chirped.

"Sorry to startle you, Miss Annie," William rasped, his twangy voice hushed. "But a telegram just come in."

Eyes wide, Annie nodded at the short, round telegraph operator. "Thank you," she managed. Her voice audibly shook, so she forced a swallow.

"Like I said, I'm mighty sorry to startle you Miss Annie, but figured you'd want it right off." William hung his balding head. "When I saw you pass by—"

Annie shook her head, shushing him. "It's no bother, William. I'll take the telegram out to Mr. Goetz." She fell in behind William on the short walk back to the tiny telegraph office.

"So is your sister ready to have that baby soon?"

Annie nodded, relishing the small talk about Katie. She couldn't wait to be an aunt, really and truly an aunt, to Katie and Peter's baby. "Fact is," Annie said, "the little one is due any day now."

"Have they chosen any names?" William held open the door to the telegraph station.

Shaking her head, Annie stepped in, suddenly anxious to post that letter to Crackerjack. "Not yet," she replied politely. "If I can take Mr. Goetz's telegram, I'll be on my way."

"Oh no Miss Annie," William explained. He pulled the door shut behind her and stepped around behind his tall wooden desk. "This telegram is for *you*."

William's voice dropped, as though he could only continue if they were shrouded in absolute secrecy. *Who could this be from*, Annie wondered as she accepted the thin piece of yellow paper from William's beefy hand.

Dear Annie stop Forgive me for not sending better news stop Hired hand Black Jack Ketchum tried to rob Broken O Ranch North here in Santa Fe stop Threw down on Crackerjack stop Crackerjack wounded but ranch safe stop Crackerjack asking for you stop Please send word if I should expect you stop
Jim Guthrie
p.s. Crackerjack asked me to tell you that he loves you stop

The small piece of life-altering yellow paper fluttered from her hand, coming to rest on the dusty wooden planks of the telegraph office floor. "Oh. Oh no," Annie breathed. The world spun around her, slow at first and then faster, as the news brought to her by way of telegram sunk in. "Crackerjack," she rasped, clinging onto the desk for support. Suddenly all the air was sucked from the room. *I can't breathe! Someone, help. Please.*

Grasping at her throat, Annie clawed at her constricting

high-necked dress. A bout of nausea washed over her in a swirling, crashing wave until she listed, her knees threatening to give way. *Crackerjack, no.*

"Miss Annie? Miss *Annie!*" William's short and squat outline furred as he rushed toward her, giving him an almost dreamlike appearance. His words sounded so far away, Annie wasn't positive if she was inside her own nightmare or if she was truly awake.

"Crackerjack," she tried to whisper again, but her muddled words were unrecognizable even to her own ears.

Before William could make it around the desk, before the obligatory prayer could find its way to the forefront of her reeling mind, before she felt her body slam against the dusty floor as the blackness came creeping, blotting and masking everything in her vision. First, the sunlight streaming through the front window of the telegraph office, then William's surprised face as he rushed to catch her.

The last thing in Annie's mind was the memory of Crackerjack's handsome face, smiling and dimpled, before it, along with everything else, simply winked out.

Sara Harris and her family have made their home in places all over the world, from the majestic Oklahoma plains to the eclectic mountains of Italy—collecting inspiration and rescue animals along the way.

Sara is a member of the Romance Writers of America, Critique Chair of RWA's Hearts Through History group, Western Fictioneers, West Houston Romance Writers, The Catholic Writer's Guild, and The Transylvanian Society of Dracula.

Sara, her romance novel-esque husband, and their children make their home in Katy, Texas. She has her BA in Medieval European History and is represented by Julie Gwinn of The Seymour Agency.

Connect with Sara online at:

www.SaraHarrisBooks.com

Also Available From

Sara Harris

House of Madness

Also Available From

WordCrafts Press

Grace Extended
    by Paula K. Parker

Fiery Red Hair, Emerald Green Eyes, and a Vicious Irish Temper
    by Ralph E. Jarrells

Angela's Treasures
    by Marian Rizzo

Until Then
    by Gail Kittleson

The Pruning
    by Jan Cline

www.WordCrafts.net